To Kill a King

Anna and Claire Trujillo

Anchorage, Alaska
www.thrivechristianpress.com

Thrive Christian Press
1120 Huffman Rd. Ste. 24-447
Anchorage, AK 99515
www.thrivechristianpress.com
authors@thrivechristianpress.com

First published by Thrive Christian Press on June 4, 2012.

ISBN: 978-0-9800600-8-9

Printed in the United States of America.

To the occupants of our home planet, whether by birth, adoption, or abduction.

~ 1 ~

My first clue that something was wrong came when my dad told me he loved me.

"You *what?*" I said.

His face reddened. "Nothing," he said hastily, withering under my shocked stare. He gave an awkward cough. "I mean, no, it's not nothing; I wanted you to know… I love you and I am proud of you." Then, before my brain could even concoct a response, he turned and rushed out of the kitchen like he couldn't wait to get away.

I dumped my now empty cereal bowl in the sink and pondered this strange incident. As far as I could remember, my father had never verbally expressed emotions such as love; he'd always been stiff and imposing, someone more comfortable giving edicts than hugs or praise. What could have prompted him to spontaneously walk into a room and announce his love for his daughter?

A sudden, sforzando boom made me spin around to see that the door had exploded in a cloud of dark smoke, and Erin Tuttle stepped into the kitchen through the empty frame.

"Guess what!" she exclaimed through the clearing smoke, flyaway waves of bright hair framing her grinning face as she brushed bits of splintered wood off her sweater. "I perfected a new bomb!"

I suppose my reaction wasn't quite as overjoyed as she'd expected, because she gave me a scrutinizing look and asked, "Is something wrong? I just made a spectacular entrance! Aren't you at least going to scream?"

I decided not to take advantage of the chance to remind her that I wasn't the type of person who screamed and chose instead to say, "You owe us a new door. My dad's going to kill me."

"Don't be preposterous. Why would he kill his only daughter? I've got a whole stack of extra doors in my garage; I'll bring one by later."

I cast an exasperated look at the demolished entryway and then followed Erin out of the house and into the cool autumn air, moving quickly so that we'd be gone by the time my dad discovered the remains of the bombed door. We climbed into Erin's car, which she had left in the driveway, and it greeted us with a welcoming hum as Erin twisted the key in the ignition. It was an obsolete model that didn't even have hover features, and the way Erin drove, it was a wonder the vehicle still ran.

Erin chattered as usual as she guided her car down the road, but today I only half listened. I stared out the window as buildings and trees zoomed past. Domina was a city-state built to impress. The main streets were smooth asphalt, the important buildings boasted facades of glistening marble, and statues and fountains decorated the gardens of expensive homes. But even the fantastic architecture couldn't distract me today.

"Erin, right before you picked me up, my dad said he loved me."

Erin snorted, and the car lurched. "He *what?*"

"I think something must be wrong."

Erin swerved tightly around a corner, narrowly missing the curb. "Parents tell their children they love them all the time, Linna. It doesn't mean the apocalypse is coming."

"This is my *dad* we're talking about. What would make him say something so weird?"

"It's obvious," said Erin, experimenting with the accelerator. "He feels guilty."

I kept facing the window, but I didn't notice the scenery anymore. "Why would he feel guilty?"

"Stop pretending you don't know what I'm talking about. I *know* you're mad at him because of what happened yesterday."

"I'm not mad."

It was a lie, and Erin saw right through it, just like she saw through everything I ever said. Sometimes it infuriated me to have a genius for a best friend, but I knew I wouldn't trade Erin for anyone else in the world.

"Okay," I admitted as Erin raised her eyebrows skeptically. "I *am* a little mad. The test all the Fighters took yesterday – I got the best score out of everyone on the written section. I would've ranked fiftieth overall if *Phil Falconer* – " I spat his name like it contained a disease – "If Phil Falconer hadn't copied my answers. He scored better than me on the other sections of the test, and because he's a lying, cheating *scoundrel* – and because my dad wouldn't change the scores even when the professors *told* him Falconer had cheated – he ranked number fifty and now I'm fifty-one."

For once, Erin didn't say anything. She just looked at the road, which I must admit greatly improved her driving.

"I guess I shouldn't be angry about one place difference," I said finally. "But out of one hundred Fighters – well, fifty is in the top half, and fifty-one is in the bottom half. I *know* I should've beaten Falconer. But my dad let him get away with it just because I'm his daughter."

"Of course he did," said Erin reasonably.

"But it doesn't make any sense! Shouldn't he be trying to *help* me?"

Erin shook her head. "Your dad is a masochist, just like you; he will always make the choice that is most painful for himself." She smiled grimly. "Like giving his own daughter a low ranking despite the fact that it's unjust."

"What do you mean, *just like me?*" I asked, surprised. But Erin was too occupied parking in the most precarious position possible to pay any attention. We slid out of the car, and I walked around the hood to stand beside Erin and peer at the sprawling mass of buildings that made up Domina's oldest and most prestigious university.

Dexter University accepted only three hundred students every year: one hundred Spies, one hundred Strategists, and one hundred Fighters. Dexter Academy's emphasis on the Three Noble Careers had helped Domina win many a war. Almost every young adult in Domina applied to Dexter Academy, and Erin and I should have felt honored to be in the tiny fraction deemed most worthy of admittance. But right now I didn't feel privileged at all.

"It's our second day here, and I'm already dreading classes," I said.

"Don't be so pessimistic," scolded Erin. "I'm thrilled for the chance to find flaws in my professors' supposedly ingenious strategies."

I shrugged and took off for the gymnasium, where the hundred new Fighters were supposed to assemble. It was all right for Erin – she was a Strategist, so all she had to worry about were books about history and manipulation techniques. But I was a Fighter, and I was not looking forward to spending every day for the rest of my education sharing workouts, training drills, and classes with a horde of competitive baboons. Including my two least favorite people in the world – a cheater named Phil Falconer and his friend Tack Breesten, who looked like a gorilla and happened to be Fighter number one.

Rows of wooden tables filled the gymnasium, providing seating for Domina's one hundred newest Fighters. Half the chairs were filled already, and Fighters were trickling into the room in clusters of two or three at a time. I slid into a seat at an empty table and noticed that the professor was already standing at the front of the room beside a large plastic bin, tapping his foot impatiently as he waited for us to settle down for the lesson.

Then I felt a jab on the back of my head. I spun around to see Tack Breesten grinning down at me. He was big and muscular with arms that seemed too long for his body, like a gorilla, and in my opinion he had social skills and intellect to match. Three rebellious tufts of coarse brown hair stood straight from his scalp where they had refused to succumb to a comb, giving the impression that three horns sprouted from his head.

"Thanks for saving us seats," he said, sliding into the chair on my left.

"Hi, Linna!" gushed Phil Falconer as he plopped down on my right. He smiled toothily at me and crossed his long, thin arms on the table in front of him. I didn't return the greeting; fury welled inside me as I noted that he didn't even show a hint of remorse for his cheating.

I scooted my chair back, about to stand to find a new place to sit, but then the professor clapped his hands and called for the Fighters' attention. Fuming, I turned my thoughts to the array of weapons that he had pulled from his bin.

"Fighters," he explained, "are the defenders of Domina, the greatest city-state since ancient Sparta. And with greatness come honor and the responsibility to defend our city-state, which is the finest since Sparta…"

He was talking in circles. I turned my attention back to the people seated on my right and left. Breesten was chewing gum loudly with a vacant look in his eyes. Falconer, on the other hand, had his eyes fixed on me, that goofy grin still plastered across his thin, hawkish features. His glasses were stuck to his temples with tape, a habit he had adopted years ago to keep them from sliding off his nose when he ran.

"Isn't this a great lesson, Linna?" he whispered, despite the fact that he wasn't listening to a word the professor said.

I ignored him and pointedly looked back at the professor, who was now holding up an archaic-looking weapon. "Does anyone know what this is?" he asked.

"I do! I do!" Falconer whispered beside me.

I raised my hand, and the professor nodded at me.

I stood to answer. "It's a rifle."

"Exactly correct. Very good, Linna."

I didn't know his name, but he knew mine. Of course he did – I was the only girl in the room. Actually, I was the first female Fighter in over a century.

Breesten shot me a nasty look as the professor beamed at me. I sat back down and pretended not to notice.

"Rifles are a type of gun," the professor continued. "Guns, though widely used in historical times, are now relics of the past. Can anyone tell me why?"

Even though I knew the answer, I didn't raise my hand this time. I didn't want to give Breesten a reason to sneer at me for being a know-it-all. None of the other Fighters volunteered to respond, so the professor answered his own question.

"Guns were highly effective weapons," he explained. "In battle, thousands could be killed from a distance with no actual man-to-man combat. The world's guns were destroyed centuries ago – when the nations disbanded into city-states – to prevent wars of mass destruction. This old-fashioned type of fighting, despite its efficiency, proved severely lacking in honor and skill. Any fool could learn to pull a trigger, but it takes a practiced warrior to wield a sword. Hand-to-hand combat is more gallant than guns, which requires only the motion of a finger on a trigger. Sword use is a skill a man may acquire only through the discipline of a true warrior."

"I can use a sword," Falconer hissed into my ear. I surreptitiously inched my chair away from him.

"It takes strict military training for a Fighter to earn the right to kill with the sword," the professor said.

"Imagine the day when you will first defend your city-state, plunging the blade through the heart of the enemy, feeling it crunch through bone and tear through muscle before finally sinking into a vital organ, such as the heart…"

I wrenched my mind away from the gruesome image and squirmed uncomfortably. Breesten had lost his blank expression, his eyes fixed intently on the professor and shining with zeal as he soaked in every word. Falconer had straightened up and muttered, "I could do that! I could do that!" to no one in particular.

"Until you have proven adept enough to be assigned a mission," the professor said as I tuned back in to his words, "you will not be given a weapon other than your own body, small explosives, and daggers."

A collective groan echoed throughout the room; apparently my classmates thought of the sword as the ultimate weapon and were reluctant to begin with other devices. Secretly, I felt a sense of relief that I wouldn't have to carry one of those sharp, deadly objects for a while. The idea of impaling a live body with the end of it – even if that body belonged to an enemy – made me feel squeamish.

Then boomed a loud knock on the gymnasium door, an authoritative knock, the kind of knock that could change a life. The professor halted his lecture as the Fighters' heads swiveled to see the door swing open and the Governor of Domina step in.

My stomach plummeted. The Governor of Domina was my dad. He was one of a triumvirate of three ministers who ruled the city-state, rotating the position of ultimate leadership – Governor – every year. This year belonged to Dad. As Governor, he was the most important person in Domina, and he considered it his obligation to ensure that I didn't get any special treatment just because I was his child. Quite the opposite, actually.

Dad's eyes found the professor's. "James, may I borrow a student for a moment?" His tongue flicked out to lick a dot of perspiration from his upper lip. "It's urgent."

I shrank down in my seat, certain my dad was going to single me out…

Then Dad said, "Tack Breesten, would you please come with me?"

Tack Breesten stood up so fast that the table shook and his chair slid across the floor with a screech. "Yes, sir!" he bellowed, and followed my dad from the room, discreetly rapping me again on the back of the head as he passed.

The professor cleared his throat. "Let us return to the lesson," he said. I tried to listen as he pulled weapon after weapon from his plastic bin and described how they worked, but I couldn't focus. I wondered why my dad had wanted to speak to Breesten. For a moment, a bizarre image of my dad ordering Breesten to make my life as miserable as possible popped into my head, but I quickly shoved it away. Dad was probably congratulating Breesten on ranking Fighter number one. Did the Governor usually take the time to fill in the top Fighter on any special responsibilities?

Phil Falconer sat slouched over the table with his chin in his hands. He scooted his chair a few inches to the left, bringing himself closer to me. I slid away from him, negating his movement. It seemed that without Breesten in the room, Falconer felt compelled to double his efforts to annoy me.

By the time the professor concluded his lecture, I had shifted to the far edge of the table and Falconer was pulled close beside me. I shot out the door and raced across the groomed university grounds to the main building, where I knew Erin's morning class should be ending. Thankfully, the Fighters had no afternoon classes today – I knew I couldn't bear another hour with Falconer or Breesten.

~

I found Erin as she was leaving class in a mob of her fellow Strategists. She was scowling.

"What's wrong?" I asked, falling into step beside her.

"The great Strategist, Perceval Tomkins, is my professor. I pointed out three major flaws in his famous battle plan for the Battle of the Hills – the fight that expanded Domina's territory about fifteen years ago – and now he spurns the sight of me."

"You know, Erin, it's probably better not to bring up the imperfections you find in esteemed Strategists' plans."

"I only told him the three *major* flaws – I didn't even mention the seventeen *minor* ones! How was your class?" Erin asked as we left the main building and headed toward the dirt field where she had left her car.

I groaned as I climbed into the passenger seat and Erin jumped behind the wheel. "How do you think? I was stuck in an airless room with ninety-nine belligerent guys and a professor who sounds like a sound track played on a loop. I don't know why –" I winced as Erin stamped the accelerator and the car shot suddenly forward – "I don't know why I thought becoming a Fighter was a good idea."

"I do," said Erin.

I rolled my eyes. Erin thought she knew everything.

"No, you don't," I said. "It was a terrible idea. Breesten and Falconer are determined to drive me insane. Well, Breesten's been determined to do that since we were five years old and started school in the same class, but Falconer… he's always been Breesten's annoying sidekick, but now he has become Master of Aggravation Number Two. He's been acting really weird."

I described his abnormal behavior during class – muttering about how smart or brave he was, staring at me with a blank grin on his face, scooting his chair closer and closer while the professor spoke…

Erin burst out laughing, and the car swerved so violently that it almost hit a lamppost.

"It's not funny!" I yelled as she managed to pull the car back onto the road.

"Yes it is," Erin said, still chuckling. "Linna, Phil Falconer is in love."

"He is? Wait – with *me*?" Panic burst like fireworks in my stomach, and it had nothing to do with Erin's driving. "But I don't want him to be in love with me! I don't even like him! You have to help me, Erin – how do I get him to leave me alone?"

Erin continued to laugh. "Why would I want him to leave you alone? This could prove useful. Plus, I find it entertaining."

The car shuddered to a halt and the engine went mute. We had pulled up alongside a sleek marble building. Flashing bulbs illuminated the doorway, where other students freshly released from class were gathered.

"What are we doing here?" I asked.

"Getting lunch," said Erin. "This is Little Dagger Café, traditional lunch-stop of Dexter University students."

I ducked low in my seat as two shadows passed through the window, both tall, but one thickly built and the other with thin limbs like muscled sticks. "Breesten and Falconer are here!" I yelped. "I'm not going in with them!"

"You don't have a choice," said Erin, "because if you don't get out of the car, I will park it in the middle of the street and cause an accident from which your mangled remains will have to be scraped with a spatula."

I reluctantly exited the car and followed Erin into the building. The blinding lights flashed to the rhythm of our footsteps as we approached a gleaming metal table. I slouched and tried to hide behind a menu as Erin swept two bright pink plastic goblets from the table and went to fill them at a fountain in a corner.

"Hey, look!" bellowed the last voice I wanted to hear. "It's Linna!"

Breesten slid onto the bench across from me, followed closely by Falconer, who said, "Hi, Linna," in a tone which I suppose could have passed as sickly sweet.

Breesten puffed out his chest impressively and said, "I bet you're wondering why the Governor pulled me out of class today."

"Not really," I admitted.

"Don't pretend you're not interested to know why your old dad wanted to speak to me," said Breesten. He raised his voice so it echoed through the entire room. "Since I am the newest number one Fighter, the Governor gave me a *mission*."

Immediately, a dozen burly boys abandoned their half-finished plates and slid into seats around my table, leaning in close to catch Breesten's every word. He seemed to swell under the attention, adopting a falsely casual air that only made his boasting more obvious.

"It's a serious mission. The Governor gave me a Strategist and everything – the best Strategist there is, Perceval Tomkins."

A surge of loyalty toward Erin made me want to say that Perceval Tomkins was only the second-best Strategist in the city-state, but I decided that Erin's ego was bloated enough already.

"Domina's under threat from Zakarra," Breesten explained, referencing a neighboring city-state. "The Second-in-Command of Zakarra contacted the Governor of Domina last night and offered him a challenge from Zakarra's King. Of course, the Governor accepted – it would be cowardly to decline."

"What's the challenge?" demanded Falconer, gazing at Breesten with wide-eyed awe behind his taped glasses.

"Technically," said Breesten, "I'm not supposed to tell you. It's highly confidential and might cause a panic if the word leaks out. But since you're all my fellow Fighters, I think the secret will be safe with you."

He lowered his voice. "I need to kill Zakarra's king."

I became aware of Erin standing beside me, a goblet of water in each hand. "That shouldn't be too hard," she said loudly. "Isn't the king of Zakarra old and ill? No one's seen him in years because he's too sick to leave his palace. You should dress in a sheet, pop out from behind his bookshelf, and say *Boo* – a good scare ought to give him a heart attack and finish him off."

Breesten scowled at her. "The palace will be heavily guarded; it won't be easy to sneak in undetected. And if I don't kill the king within three days, there will be *consequences*."

Falconer shuddered sycophantically. "What kind of consequences, Tack?"

Breesten beamed at the Fighters gathered around him, relishing the attention. "If I succeed," he said, "Zakarra will surrender to Domina's control. But if I fail..." The way he said it made it very obvious that he thought his failure was highly unlikely. "If I fail, Domina will be forced to surrender to Zakarra, and the Governor will have to sacrifice one of our citizens to be publicly executed in Zakarra as a sign of Domina's submission."

"Who?" Erin demanded, setting down the goblets on the table so hard that water sloshed over the rims.

"He didn't say," said Breesten mysteriously. "But you can see that this is a *very* important mission. Lives hang in the balance."

"One life," corrected Erin. "Only one person will die. The king, or..."

Interrupting her with a great sigh to exemplify the weight of responsibility that had been thrust upon him, Breesten stood up and walked over to a soda fountain, signaling the end of the discussion. Falconer scurried after him, and the other Fighters returned to their tables, muttering excitedly among themselves.

"Let's leave, Linna," said Erin. "I'm not hungry anymore."

"Me neither," I said. "Seeing Breesten usually ruins my appetite."

We left our goblets on the table and exited through the flashing doors. Erin fumbled with the key as she unlocked her car, and her driving was worse than usual. I was jittery from near-crashes by the time we finally pulled into my driveway.

We walked in through the blown-up door. The house was empty and silent as we entered the kitchen. I found a scrap of paper with slanted writing on the counter and picked it up. "*Linna*," I read aloud, "*your friend Erin had better fix the door before I get home tonight, or I will volunteer you to clean Domina's public restrooms.*"

"I'll bring another door later," Erin promised. She took the paper from me and tossed it into the trash.

I dug in the pantry and found a loaf of bread. "Want a sandwich?" I asked Erin, stacking cheese on a slice.

"No, I told you I'm not hungry."

"I wasn't either, but now that I am free of Breesten's presence, my appetite has miraculously returned." I stuck the sandwich in the toaster oven and leaned against the counter, watching the cheese melt. Erin chewed on her thumbnail and watched me with a thoughtful expression.

"Thinking deep thoughts?" I asked.

"You have no idea," she said. "There's an obligation for profoundness when gifted with brains such as mine."

I opened the toaster oven and slid my lunch onto a plate. The sticky yellow cheese left hot grease on my fingers, and I wiped them on a dishtowel to clean them off. Erin slid my homework from my bag and did it for me as I ate. Usually she talked nonstop, but right now she was strangely taciturn, and I chewed and watched her hand guide the pencil scratchily over a page.

When I'd put my plate away and Erin had set down my pencil, she stood up. "I'd better go," she said. "I'll be back this evening with a new door. Are you okay here by yourself?"

"Of course I am. I'm not a little kid anymore, you know."

Erin shrugged and handed me my freshly finished homework. "I did it in your handwriting so your professor won't know you got help. And I got a couple questions wrong on purpose so that he won't wonder where your sudden intelligence sprang from."

"Thanks," I said. "But I could've done it myself."

"And waste an evening torturing yourself by describing old weapons? This is what I mean when I call you a masochist."

I sat at the kitchen table, staring at my homework and trying to find which questions Erin had answered incorrectly so I could fix them, but the only thing I could think about was Breesten's mission. I hadn't known that my dad had accepted a challenge from Zakarra's king. The king must have felt pretty confident about his security if he had invited a Dominan Fighter to try to assassinate him – Dominan Fighters were infamous as the best of any city-state in the world.

Despite Erin's pretenses, I knew that Breesten's mission was of great magnitude. If he failed, it would mean the end of Domina's centuries-long reign as the strongest city-state in the region, and an innocent citizen would lose his or her life. For a moment I tried to imagine whom my dad would sacrifice, trying to put myself inside my father's mind.

Then Erin's words from this morning floated into my head. *"Your dad is a masochist, just like you; he will always make the choice that is most painful for himself."*

And my dad's words chased them. *"I wanted you to know... I love you and I am proud of you."*

That was when I realized that I was going to die.

~ 2 ~

I'd decided I wanted to become a Fighter over a year ago, and since then the aim of all my training had been to make me strong, brave, and coolheaded even while clasped in death's brutal jaws. But right now I didn't feel courageous at all; I felt stunned, like someone had whacked me on the head and the world was refusing to come back into focus.

One part of my mind told me not to be ridiculous – my father would never hand me over for public execution. But the other part of my brain – the coldly logical, unfeeling part I had inherited from my dad – admitted that sacrificing me made perfect sense. If I died, my dad would suffer greatly, but he wouldn't have to rip someone else's family apart. He wouldn't have to watch another parent weeping for a slaughtered child or endure the curses of a citizen whose spouse or sibling had been snatched away. All the pain would crush his heart, not someone else's.

"Linna, I'm back! Come help me put this door in!" Erin's voice signaled her return. I was still sitting at the table, staring at my empty plate, trying to swallow the panic that threatened to overwhelm me.

"Erin," I said quietly.

"Do you have a screwdriver somewhere, Linna?"

"Erin."

"Oh, I found it. Come on – I can't hold the door up and screw this in at the same time."

"Erin, I'm going to die."

There was a long, stretched pause, and then Erin said with perceptibly strained cheerfulness, "Of course you are. It's called *mortality*."

"No," I said, "I think my dad is going to have me publicly executed in Zakarra."

"Don't be preposterous," said Erin, heaving the heavy wooden door upright and shoving it into position. "He'll only hand you over to the Zakarrans if Breesten fails, which isn't going to happen." The way she said this told me that she'd figured out whom my dad planned to forfeit long ago.

"But what if he *does* fail?"

Erin snorted. "His mission is so simple he should be able to do it in his sleep. Listen, Linna, I figured out hours ago that your dad will probably sacrifice you if the king isn't killed, but I'm positive that Breesten will carry out his mission and everything will be all right. Besides, Tomkins is his Strategist, and Tomkins is the best."

"You said that you found three major flaws and seventeen minor flaws in his strategy at the Battle of the Hills."

Erin shrugged. "He still won the battle… the victory just came with unnecessary casualties." Despite her bravado, I caught the tremor in her voice. She tossed me the screwdriver. "Now will you help me with this?"

I began screwing the hinges into the frame so forcefully that Erin said, "Careful, don't break it!" I slowed down my hands, my mind a blank, and tried to believe that Breesten would fulfill his mission. But a seed of doubt pinched at the back of my mind, refusing to yield to the optimism Erin was trying to lend me.

"Erin, can you give me a ride to the Triumvirate Building? I'm going to ask my dad to let me help kill the king."

Erin laughed scornfully. "That's a terrible idea, Linna. You could never kill anyone."

Now anger was replacing the cold fear I had felt earlier. "I'm a Fighter, Erin. I'm being trained to kill. Yesterday I beat up a dummy until it fell to pieces and its head and stomach burst open."

"Yeah, and old newspapers poured out," said Erin. "That wasn't real."

"They were cotton balls," I corrected her. I bit my lip and wrenched the last screw into place.

Erin gave the door an experimental swing and nodded in approval. Then she pushed it open and gestured for me to step outside. I obeyed.

As I climbed into Erin's car, I realized how unfair it was that I might die in less than three days without even learning how to drive. Maybe Erin would give me a lift to my execution. I sat in stony silence, alternating waves of terror and determination washing over me, until we screeched to a halt outside the Triumvirate Building.

"I don't think you should mention the mission to your dad," Erin said, putting a hand out to stop me from leaving the vehicle. "It's top-secret – Breesten wasn't supposed to tell anyone. You'll get him in trouble, and it will sound like you're accusing your dad of planning your murder."

"But Breesten *deserves* to get in trouble and my dad *is* planning my murder."

Erin chewed her lip, and I watched as the worried furrow in her brow faded away like a cloud swept aside to unblock the sun, leaving a familiar look of beaming confidence in her eyes. "Trust me," she said, "I have an infallible plan."

~

I trusted Erin and didn't doubt her brilliance, but every time she came up with a plan, it seemed too absurd to work. This one was no different.

"Are you sure about this?" I asked Erin, passing through the building's security sensors without incident. This was Domina's highest government building, and the triumvirate wanted to make sure that no one entered it with a sword or bomb in his or her jacket. I didn't see how that would help keep anyone safe should someone choose to murder one of the triumvirate – Dominan Fighters could kill just as easily with a fist as with a blade.

I knew where Dad's office was. He had often taken me to work with him when I was small and let me lay on his carpet with a sketchpad and packet of crayons while he ran the city-state. I stopped before the smooth, black door with its metal nameplate, which read *Governor Neil Nichols*. I looked at Erin, who nodded encouragingly, and pushed open the door.

Dad looked up. He looked pale and had his fingers on his temples as though trying to suppress a persistent headache, elbows resting on his paper-strewn desk. "Linna?" he said. "And Erin? What are you doing here?"

I took a deep breath, and, feeling like a fool, asked, "Dad, we were wondering what you would like for breakfast."

"Breakfast – *what?* – it's late afternoon, Linna."

I brazenly plowed on. Stick to the plan, Erin had said, stick to the plan and nothing will go wrong. "The chef would like to recommend roasted gorilla; it is deliciously succulent and cooked to perfection…"

"I don't have time for games!" Dad roared.

"Served with mushrooms…" I continued.

"No! No, I don't want this roasted gorilla with mushrooms, or whatever it is, just leave me alone!"

"The chef has received countless compliments for this recipe," interrupted Erin. "Julius Caesar enjoyed it so much that he ordered it made for him five times a week. Other notable eaters of this delicacy include long-lived Methuselah, great conqueror Genghis Khan, Dominan founder Nancy Dexter, and honored current Fighter Tack Breesten."

"Breesten said the meal's on him," I said, heart drumming.

"Tack Breesten is in on this prank, too?" Dad fumed. "He of all people should know that I'm too busy for such nonsense, especially now…"

He trailed off, and I leapt onto his words like an owl pouncing a mouse. "What do you mean, Dad?"

"Nothing!" he bellowed. "Look, I have a critical meeting in ten minutes, and I can't afford to waste any more time."

"If you choose the roasted gorilla, Tack wanted you to give him one of your mushrooms," said Erin. "He said something about how it would go well with his mission."

"Wait," I said, spinning on Erin and pretending to recoil, "Did you just say that Tack Breesten has a *mission?* Is this true, Dad?"

Dad's cheeks flushed with anger as all the blood rushed to his face. "How do you know about that? You're not supposed to know about that!"

According to Erin's plan, what I was supposed to say now was, "*Okay, I know, what are you going to do about it, kill me?*" Then Dad was supposed to break down and tell me everything, and while he was flooded with guilt Erin would persuade him to let me accompany Breesten on his mission to make sure the king really did die within three days. But all I could choke out was, "Okay, I know…" Then my gaze slipped from Dad's eyes and down to the floor like I couldn't hold it up any longer.

The opportunity was lost, and I knew it. So did Erin, judging by the disappointed look on her face. Dad jumped to his feet, yelling, "Out, *out!*" Erin and I rushed from the room and watched my dad slam the door hard enough to make his nameplate fall off.

Erin glared at me.

"I'm sorry," I said miserably.

"What did I tell you?" Erin said. "I told you to *stick to the plan*! What part of *stick to the plan* don't you understand, Linna? I told you to *trust* me!"

"I'm sorry!" I said again.

Erin sighed. "My plans would always work perfectly if people just *followed* them. Well, it's too late now – at least we tried."

I stared at the black door, stubbornly shut, closing me off. I wanted to kick it, knock it from its hinges, and force my dad to talk to me. I couldn't remember ever being so angry before, not even yesterday when

Falconer had cheated and usurped my rightful position as Fighter fifty. Erin was saying, "Don't worry; I'll think up another plan," as she ushered me down the hall and into the atrium, where a white marble statue depicting three figures towered under a lofty glass ceiling – a Strategist holding a clipboard, a Spy with spectacles half-raised to his face, and a Fighter wielding a sword, all standing shoulder-to-shoulder.

I looked into the Fighter's eyes, hoping to see something in them, but they were cold and unforthcoming, made of nothing more than hard, dead stone.

Erin suddenly grabbed my arm. "It's Breesten!" she hissed.

I peered around the statue and saw that Breesten was indeed swaggering through the Triumvirate Building's front doors, his broad, long arms gesticulating as he spoke with the white-haired man beside him.

"That's Perceval Tomkins," said Erin. "He and Breesten are probably meeting with your dad to outline how to carry out the mission." Her grip on my arm tightened. "Linna, go tell Breesten to do a good job on his mission."

"What? No – I don't want to talk to him."

"But if he fails, you might be executed."

"No!"

"Fine," said Erin, "I'll tell him myself." And before I could stop her she had slipped around the statue and was heading toward Breesten and Tomkins with a strut to put Breesten's to shame.

"Tack!" she called, and Breesten and the Strategist both looked up. "Listen to me, Breesten," said Erin, standing right in front of him and glowering so ferociously that Breesten squirmed. "You'd better not fail your mission, because if you do, my best friend might die." Then she marched back to me as Breesten and Tomkins stared after her in befuddlement.

"Come on, Linna," she said. "Let's go. There's nothing else we can do here." She pushed me past the security sensors, through the polished marble entry, and out the doors to the parking lot. A strong breeze had begun, and the air smelled slightly salty, like rain was imminent.

I took deep gulps of that air, trying to fit in as many breaths as possible, wondering if I would still be alive to enjoy it in three days. It was so frustrating that there was nothing I could do, no way to know for certain that Breesten wouldn't screw up. I was powerless. All I could do was hope desperately that Breesten, possibly my least favorite person in the world, would succeed in his mission.

We climbed back into Erin's ancient car, and she drove to a nearby convenience store and pulled into its parking lot. The sky was beginning to darken now. Shadows swooped in through the windshield as we sat, staring at the swaying trees and gentle raindrops.

I wondered why we hadn't driven back to my house, but I didn't ask. I much preferred sitting next to my best friend to pacing the halls alone in a quiet, empty house. Erin was uncharacteristically reticent, chewing on a strand of flame-colored hair, her eyes gleaming thoughtfully.

I decided to break the silence. "I still want to help with the mission."

Erin frowned. "Your dad will never allow it."

I laughed, even though nothing seemed very funny. "What more can he do? He's already going to kill me."

"And you could never kill the king," said Erin. "This is a job that's best left to Breesten. He's brutal enough to actually carry it out."

"But he doesn't know how much is at stake!" I protested. "I wouldn't put it past Breesten to *deliberately* fail. He's always despised me – I bet he thinks it would be hilarious if I died."

"He doesn't want you dead," said Erin calmly. "And he's too eager to prove himself to blight his first mission."

"I don't trust him," I said. "And I don't trust his Strategist either. Everyone thinks Tomkins is the best, but you found twenty mistakes in his most famous battle plan. I'm scared that – I think – what if they're not good enough?" I watched Erin chewing her hair and saw the anxiety through her impression of composure, flaring with fear at the thought that she might lose her best friend. "I'm going to carry out Breesten's mission for him," I said. "I'm going to kill the king, and I'll need your help."

"*My* help?" said Erin. "I'm a Strategist, not a Fighter."

"Exactly," I said. "I need you to concoct a foolproof strategy to get me out of class tomorrow so that I can go to Zakarra and kill the king for myself. And I need you to play hooky too, because I'll need you to drive me there."

Erin gazed at me in reverence. "I think you've finally lost your marbles."

"I haven't gone crazy," I insisted. "My life is at stake, and you're the best Strategist I know." I met her eyes and pleaded, "Please, Erin. I would do the same for you."

To my relief, a roguish smirk spread over Erin's face and she said, "Linna, I think this is the craziest – and the best – idea you've ever had."

She let out a jubilant whoop as the car careened wildly out of the parking lot, and I wondered if it was really wise to count myself fortunate to have the aid of a person whose hobby was playing with bombs.

It was very late now, and the sky overhead glittered with stars like many eyes, keeping watch over the city-state as it slept. Erin and I both knew where Falconer lived; as young children we had been invited to his house for birthday parties and play dates, before Breesten had developed his cutthroat personality and Falconer had become his sidekick. It seemed strange to think that not many years ago we had laughed together and bashed at piñatas, arguing over which slice of cake had the most frosting. We were all grown up now, but I didn't feel any more mature than the little kid I remembered daring Phil to blow out all his candles in one huff. I'd read that in the old days, people had not been considered adults until they were older than I was now. That seemed like a smart system to me. I'd much rather be a kid right now, oblivious to everything, instead of a newly-fledged adult who knew she might have less than three days left to live.

Erin pulled the car up Falconer's driveway and parked in front of the stately brick house. "Go knock on the door and see if he's home," she said.

"What about you?" I asked.

"I'll wait in the car. He'll listen to you – he's your boyfriend, after all."

"Say that again and I'll punch you," I warned.

"No you won't."

"Yes, I will."

She said it again. I didn't punch her. I tried to ignore her *I-told-you-so* expression as I climbed out of the car and ascended the Falconers' front steps.

Phil answered on my fifth knock, a stack of toast in one hand and cheeks bulging. "Linna!" he squawked, and crumbs sprayed down his shirt. He chewed and swallowed. "I wasn't expecting you."

I decided not to prolong the conversation. "Yeah, well, I need your help. Come on out – Erin Tuttle's waiting in the car – she'll explain better than I can."

"Yeah! Sure!" Dreamy-eyed, Falconer tossed his toast away and followed me down the steps. He was acting like a complete fool; as I climbed into the car beside Erin and Falconer took the backseat, I swore to never fall in love.

Erin got straight to business. "Okay, Phil, let's make this quick," she said. "Linna needs help, and we were wondering if we can trust you."

"Yeah, of course you can trust me," said Falconer.

"Good," said Erin. "Linna won't be at university tomorrow. If a professor or anyone notices, you need to tell them she's sick, all right?"

"Linna's sick, got it," Falconer repeated. "But where'll you be, Linna?"

"I can't tell you that," I said.

"Tack's not going to be there because of his mission… do you have a mission, too?"

"Sort of," I said.

"Cool," said Falconer. "You must be really amazing to get a mission even though you're only number fifty-one. Wouldn't the second mission usually go to Fighter number two?"

I gritted my teeth. "Bye, Phil," I said pointedly, and he had no choice but to climb out the car door. As Erin backed down the driveway and sped away, I caught a glimpse of Falconer in the rearview mirror, his taped glasses reflecting Erin's taillights and a sappy grin slopped across his face as he gazed wistfully after the retreating car.

~ 3 ~

I woke up the next morning with nervousness heaving in my stomach. For a moment, I considered not getting out of bed and trying to sleep through what might be my last full day of life. But then I remembered my unauthorized mission and forced my weary body out from under the covers.

Dad was in the kitchen by the time I arrived downstairs for breakfast. There were dark half-circles shadowing his eyes, and his face was paler than usual. For a moment, I almost felt a twinge of sympathy for him, but then I remembered that he had chosen me to die. I steeled my emotions and marched to the pantry for some cereal.

I could feel his eyes on me as I poured my breakfast into a bowl. I kept my back stubbornly turned toward him, almost afraid to meet his eyes. I was afraid of what I might find there – would his expression read fear? Pity? Or would he remain stony, unreadable, unfeeling…

Dad cleared his throat. I pointedly did not look up as I carried my bowl of cereal to the table and began spooning bites into my mouth. My stomach ached with nerves, but I refused to surrender to the dread.

"Linna," my dad said brusquely.

Now I had no choice but to acknowledge him. "Yes?"

He cleared his throat again, as if trying to find something to say. "How's school?"

"Fine," I said, keeping my tone curt. I lifted another bite to my mouth, but before I could eat it, he spoke again.

"Listen, Linna," he said. "I know you're upset that I gave Phil Falconer a better place than you, but – "

I cut him off. "I don't care. It's over." Falconer's cheating during our test was probably the least of my concerns right now.

He didn't say anything for a moment, then heaved himself from his seat with unnecessary effort. "Well then," he said, "have a good day."

He waited for my response, but I didn't offer one. What could I say? I doubted that anything good would come of my day, unless I managed to kill the king, but I was trying not to think about that until the time came.

"Um, see you after school," Dad said, and then he rushed out of the kitchen. I heard him clomp up the stairs to his bedroom and almost wished that I had been a little less abrupt with him. But it was too late to change that now.

Today Erin opened the door instead of blowing it up, a considerate decision for which I was grateful. "Everything's going smoothly so far," she said. "Falconer will tell the professors you're sick, so no one will think twice of your absence until three-thirty this afternoon at the earliest, as long as they don't contact your dad. I bribed my younger brother with cookies to deliver notes to all my professors individually telling them that I have switched out of their classes, so no one should realize that I'm not in Domina, either. I'll fill you in on the rest of the plan as we drive."

Zakarra was almost twenty-five kilometers away from Domina, so Erin had plenty of time to tell me her plan. It didn't sound that impressive to me.

"So I'm supposed to go in, find the palace, and figure out how to sneak inside?" I asked. "You're a Strategist and a genius, and that's all you could come up with?"

"There's more," Erin insisted, taking her hands off the wheel to dig in her pocket. She pulled out a crumpled photograph and handed it to me. I unfolded it to see a faded image of a pale-eyed old man with a curly gray beard. "That's King Gerald," said Erin. "He's the one you need to kill."

"He looks nice," I said, staring into his sad, pale eyes. "I don't want to *kill* him."

"Sorry, friend, but you have no choice; assassination is what you signed up for. Now, I snuck into Tomkin's office last night and found the file on Breesten's mission. Dominan spies stationed in Zakarra are confident that King Gerald has not left his palace. Either his security is far more advanced than anything we've ever seen, or he's like a bug on a bull's eye waiting to be smashed to a smear."

"Ugh," I groaned. "Promise me to never use that bug comparison again." I forced myself to rip my eyes away from King Gerald's face.

Erin went on as if she hadn't heard me. "Zakarra is a walled city. There are four gates, situated on the north, south, east, and west sides of the city. I have eliminated these gates as points of entrance because they will undoubtedly be solidly guarded."

"It's a walled city?" I said. "How's that going to help protect it from intruders? All you'd need is a helicopter to get over the walls."

"Unfortunately, as we are operating behind the government's back, we don't even have a toy helicopter at our disposal," Erin snapped. "Besides, the king probably has a unit watching the skies."

"I was just making a point," I said defensively. "So, if we can't use the gates and we can't fly over the walls, how are we going to get in?"

Erin half smiled. "Let's figure that out when we get there."

We rolled over a crest of a hill, and suddenly I saw Zakarra spread before us like a walled beast lurking in a landscape of trees. Without warning, Erin veered the car off the road and started plowing through the forest.

"Hey!" I yelled as a pine branch whacked my window and sticks crunched under the tires like dry, snapping bones. "What're you doing?"

"Hiding the car," Erin explained, looking like she was enjoying herself way too much as she wove between tree trunks. On each bump, I felt my brain slosh in my skull, and I worried it might liquefy if Erin didn't slow down soon. "We can go the rest of the way on foot."

After making sure the car was parked well out of sight of the road, we trekked off in the direction of the city-state. It was warm for autumn, and the bright orange leaves overhead made this seem more like an adventure out of a fairytale than real life, but I was too afraid to let myself forget what lay at stake. I wanted to run to the city at a full sprint, kill the king, and get this over with, but I knew that I couldn't leave Erin behind.

I needed her; I needed her brains; without her I didn't even have a clue how to get into Zakarra.

Finally we reached the wall. Erin's forehead glinted with sweat from our hike. I was sweating too, but not from the walk or the heat – my whole body felt clammy at the thought of what I was preparing to do.

"How do we get in?" I asked, rapping the sturdy brick wall. It was obviously too high and too thick to scale, and the soil beneath it was too hard-packed and rocky for digging, even if we'd happened to bring shovels.

Erin chewed her knuckle in concentration, examining the seemingly impenetrable structure. "Let's look for a good place to get in," she said. "I'll go this way; you go that way." She tore away through the trees to the left.

I stared after her, at a loss of what to look for, and then took off to the right, examining the wall without an inkling of what Erin wanted me to find.

Then Erin's yell cut through the woods. I ran to her side to find her grinning at a stretch of weathered bricks. "This is our perfect entrance point," she said. "The bricks here are old and slightly crumbled, and I don't hear any sounds of activity from the other side. I've planted a bomb to break through the wall. It should detonate in about ten seconds."

Bomb?

I gaped at her, horrified, and she laughed at my expression. "Relax, it's only a little bomb."

"What do you mean, it's only a little – "

BOOM!

Dust and smoke flew in all directions as the wall almost exploded; I dove to the ground, pinning Erin under me, holding my arms over my head in an attempt to shield us both from flying chunks of brick. Finally debris stopped raining down and I dared to lift my head, coughing on gunpowder-scented dust.

I yanked Erin to her feet. "Are you insane?"

"Maybe," Erin admitted, unable to control her enormous grin. "But look – you're *in!*"

She pointed to the gaping hole in the wall. Through it I saw a grimy, rust-covered dumpster blocking a twisted alleyway beyond.

"Here," said Erin, pressing something small and rectangular into my palm.

"It's a two-way texter," I said, holding it up to see the small screen and minute keyboard.

"I've got the other," said Erin. "I'll be waiting in the car; we'll use this to communicate. Today you're doing surveillance only, so nothing should go wrong, but if you get into any trouble, tell me right away and I'll figure out a way to rescue you."

I nodded my thanks and squeezed Erin's arm, trying to communicate more in that squeeze than I knew I ever could with words. Then I walked over to the newly made opening in the wall, hoisted myself over the dumpster, and waved goodbye to my closest, truest friend in the world.

"Good luck!" Erin called after me. I stuffed the two-way texter into my pocket, brushed my hair from my eyes, and set off down the narrow, winding Zakarran alley. With every step, I prayed that I was not approaching my doom. Now that I was actually in Zakarra, this seemed like a very bad idea. The city-state was huge – and if all the streets were as snaky and claustrophobic as this, I could explore for days and never even lay eyes on the palace.

But then the alley spilled out onto a broad, busy street, and I got my first good look at Zakarra – the city-state where, if both Breesten and I failed, I might die.

If Domina was grand and well designed, Zakarra was a jumble of new ideas built on top of the old. The streets were narrower than the ones I was used to, permitting cars to rumble down alongside strolling pedestrians laden with briefcases or shopping bags. The larger buildings were clean and impressive, but squished between them stood rickety brick or wooden structures, sometimes one or two built on top of another. I saw two beggars sitting on opposite sides of the road, competing with each other for the coins tossed by passersby.

Voices flew around me like crisscrossing projectiles, calling and babbling in a rolling accent that I had never heard in Domina.

Great – why hadn't anyone warned me about the accent? I'd give myself away if I so much as opened my mouth to speak.

I felt conspicuous, like I'd stumbled into a foreign world, and I was surprised and relieved when nobody seemed to look at me twice. I reminded myself of my mission. Palace…where was the palace? I knew that I needed to make the most of every second. Choosing a direction at random, I let my shoes slap the crowded road and took off at a jog in search of the palace.

After searching for nearly an hour, I was certain that I was running in the wrong direction. The streets were growing narrower, the buildings shabbier, and the people more hunched and despondent; this was obviously a slum, and I assumed that the palace would be in a better-looking part of the city-state.

I slowed to a walk and pulled the texter that Erin had given me from my pocket. I tapped out a message: *I can't find the palace.*

After a pause, Erin's words popped up on the tiny screen. *Ask a Zakarran. They'll know where it is.*

I crinkled up my forehead and stowed away the texter. The Zakarrans strolling the street around me walked with their heads low, their shoulders stooped as though bearing an invisible, burdensome load. Nobody even glanced at me as they scurried past, carrying grocery bags or crying children.

None of them seemed like the enemy I had imagined; they were merely ordinary, weary people trying to stumble through existence, just like me. But none of their lives depended on killing someone.

I had no idea how to ask someone here for directions. For one thing, associating with citizens of the city that might lead to my demise made me feel sick to my stomach. And for another, my Dominan accent would surely expose me as an outsider. I didn't want to end up thrown in jail or dead… though I reminded myself that it was possible I would be dead soon anyway.

I flagged down a passing boy. He didn't seem intimidating at all – small, wiry, with dirty streaks smeared across his face. He had wide set green eyes and dark, auburn hair that reminded me of Erin.

"Excuse me," I said, trying to imitate the up-and-down tones of the Zakarran accent, "I must have taken a wrong turn. Do you know the way to the palace?"

He narrowed his eyes in suspicion. "The palace? Why d'you want to go there?"

Now my heart was beating quickly in my chest. *Think!* I ordered myself. I wished that Erin was right beside me, her ingenious mind inventing flawless plans and elaborate explanations. But it was I – Linna – and I didn't have a clue what to say.

"Um…" As my tongue fumbled for the words, the boy cut in.

"Did you hear that someone's going to try and kill King Gerald?"

"No," I said, my palms beginning to sweat. "Who?"

"No idea." He flashed a quick grin at me. Then he leaned closer and lowered his voice so that only I could hear. "But I almost wish that someone *would* kill him. Know what I mean?"

I shook my head a little too quickly. "No! No, I don't know."

He shrugged and ran off, calling over his shoulder, "Keep going straight! You'll see the palace soon enough."

I followed the boy's directions, breaking into a quicker stride despite the cramping in my legs and the fact that my sweat was already sticking my shirt to my back. I wanted to find the palace and get out of this city-state as quickly as I could.

But the street seemed to go on for an eternity, passing cramped, shabby houses, sleek, metallic office buildings, and raised car lots full of vehicles of all shapes and sizes. Maybe it had been a mistake to embark on this mission; perhaps my dad was right to think that Breesten and Tomkins could kill the king and I was a fool to think otherwise, to take matters into my own hands.

But I reminded myself that it was *my* life on the line, not one of theirs. The self-assurance Breesten had shown when given the mission was not a sign that he would succeed; it was an indication that he hadn't taken his role seriously enough. To him, this was just a chance to enlarge his self-importance and earn fame, but for me this mission was the difference between life and death.

I began to think that the redheaded boy had given me misleading directions; the buildings didn't look any grander now than they had five blocks ago, and the people still looked stooped and unhappy. I decided I didn't like Zakarra very much.

Then a hand slammed down on my shoulder. I didn't speak – I didn't think – it was like my body acted before my mind, like my Fighter training took complete control of my body. I slung my right arm behind me, pinning a hard, skeletal body against my back, and crunched forward so that the body flew over my head and landed on the ground in front of me. My fist flew up, poised to hammer down, to strike, to smash, to kill…

But then I came to my senses and took a closer look at the figure at my mercy. She was old, with stringy gray hair and eyes wild with fear, sprawled painfully on the ground where I'd thrown her with her limbs strewn out.

Shocked at what I'd nearly done, I unclenched my raised fist and pulled her to her feet. "I'm sorry," I stammered. "I didn't mean to attack you." I felt shaken, like I was the one who'd been hurled to the ground. My instincts had taken over before I'd had time to think, to restrain myself; it was like I had turned into a machine that was programmed to kill. Was that what I was becoming – a monster who acted without thought or emotion? Was my training squeezing compassion out of me, replacing whatever it was that made me human?

The woman peered at me. The fear had gone out of her eyes; now they were calm, limpid, and a very pale blue. She pulled her hand from my grasp and smoothed out her jacket, then said, "A coin for your fortune?"

I blinked.

"I'll tell you your fortune," the woman said, grinning to reveal that she was missing her front teeth. She grabbed the front of my shirt and pulled me close to her face, lowering her voice as if telling me a great secret. *"I can see the future!"*

I pulled her hands away from me and took a step back. "I don't want to know my fortune." I tried to slip around her, but she spread out her arms like bat wings and advanced, forcing me back into the shadow of a brick building. My shoulder blades brushed a hard wall.

"Come on," the old woman said, leering, her voice high and hoarse. "Let me see your destiny; let me have my fun – and your fee will pay for my dinner tonight!"

I could have knocked her over and ran, but that seemed like a poor way to express my apologies to an old lady I had just nearly killed. I dug in my pocket and felt a single coin there, not even enough for a stick of gum. I pulled it out. "Sorry, this is all I have," I said. "I don't think it's enough."

"It's enough! It's enough!" the fortuneteller cawed. She snatched at the coin, but I pulled it away.

"I don't want to know my fortune," I said again. I didn't know why my heart was beating so loudly, but I felt like something cold and constricting was squeezing my chest. "How about I give you the coin in exchange for directions to the palace?"

Her pale eyes stared into my face like she might find something valuable there, and finally she gave a slow nod. She held out her hand. As soon as I set my coin in her palm, her bony fingers curled over it and she stuffed it greedily into her grungy jacket. "Keep walking that way," she said, jerking her head in the direction I'd been heading. "You'll find the palace."

"Thank you," I said gratefully, pushing away from the wall behind me and starting to walk away.

But she flung out a hand to stop me. "Wait – " she said, "Your fortune…"

I shoved her away. "I don't want to know!" And I tore down the road.

But even at my fastest sprint, the wind whistling past my ears couldn't drown out the words she yelled after me. "You are doomed to die!"

~ 4 ~

I stopped to breathe, sides aching and sweat dribbling down the back of my neck. My heart hammered at a rapid tempo, and not only from the effort of running. The old fortuneteller's words ricocheted through my mind.

I sucked in air, wondering suddenly why I'd never realized how miraculous my lungs were before. They felt so fragile now as I thought of death, like two balloons that could burst at the slightest impact. I struggled to keep the metallic taste of fear from rising in my throat. I didn't want to die.

I pulled out my texter, planning to send a terrified message to Erin describing the woman's chilling prediction, but then I thought better of it and stowed the texter back in my pocket. I knew that Erin would only laugh off the fortuneteller's prophecy that I was going to die. *"Of course you are; it's called mortality,"* she would say. Erin didn't believe in fortunetellers. Neither did I, actually, but I couldn't shake away the stone of dread that had settled in my stomach.

I wondered how I would be executed. The thought of spears piercing holes in my body or a sword slicing off my head only intensified my panic. I hoped for a quick death. But even if an axe sliced my head neatly off, would there be a few moments of immeasurable agony before my consciousness flickered out? Or would I spiral into oblivion before the pain registered in my brain?

Don't think about it, I ordered myself. Focus on the mission. I lifted my gaze off of the cracked asphalt street and found the palace right in front of me. If squalor defined what I'd seen of Zakarra, the palace was a radiant gem planted in the center of a compost heap. Surrounded by a five-foot wall imbedded with colored shards of tiles to form a bright mosaic, it rose several stories from the ground like a majestic marble mountain with a flat stone roof. Green tips of trees and the spray of fountains protruded from behind the wall, surrounding the building.

I quickly reached for my texter and sent an update to Erin. *I found the palace. It's surrounded by a wall. Now what?*

Find the entrance, Erin replied.

Trying to look casual, I walked around the palace's perimeter. On the east side of the palace I found a pair of ornate iron gates, guarded by three stiffly standing guards in scarlet uniforms.

Found them, I texted Erin. *They're guarded.* I wanted to add that this was hopeless, but I shoved that thought away. Erin did not appreciate pessimism.

A hand clamped down on my arm with such force that I thought my feet would sink through the pavement and into the earth. I tensed but didn't attack; I had learned my lesson with the fortuneteller.

"What," said a frustratingly familiar voice, "are you doing in Zakarra?"

I spun around to see Tack Breesten glaring at me; now I almost wished I *had* punched him. "I'm looking for a way into the palace," I answered truthfully. There was no point in bluffing. What else could I possibly be here for?

His face darkened with anger. He leaned close to me and snarled, "This is *my* mission, Linna, not yours, and I don't want you ruining it for me." His fingers twitched as though itching to curl into a fist and wallop me in the face, but he just managed to contain himself.

"I don't want to ruin your mission," I explained. Rage stormed across his features as I spoke; it was obvious he thought I'd come to steal his glory.

"Then why are you here? Just because your dad's the Governor it doesn't mean you have to…"

I held up a hand to silence him and nodded pointedly at our surroundings. A few Zakarran residents had already glanced interestedly in our direction, and it would be catastrophic to expose our intentions in front of them. Breesten clamped his mouth shut and scowled at me like I'd just stolen his Christmas present.

I turned away, furious with myself for letting Breesten discover me, and broodingly watched the streams of Zakarrans as they walked purposefully down the streets. Some looked like they were on their way to work, some looked like they had just finished shopping, and a few children – most likely truants – scampered through the crowds as they played a rowdy form of tag. Once in a while a car rolled past, and I noticed that all the vehicles were at least as old as Erin's, beat-up and lacking hover features.

As I watched, a man with a briefcase in hand passed before the palace gates, turned his head toward the palace, and spat at the base of the wall. Then he brushed off his shabby coat and stalked on with his head held high.

"Listen," Breesten hissed, lowering his voice, "I don't know how you got into this city or what you think you're doing here, but the fact that you're messing around with my first assignment is absolutely unacceptable."

I glowered at him, too filled with resentment to reply. This wasn't just his precious mission; my life was at stake. I tried to step away, but he only intensified his grip on my arm.

"How did you get in?" he demanded. "Did your dad bring you?"

"No," I admitted. "Erin blew up part of the wall."

"Erin!" Breesten said disdainfully. "I bet you have her thinking up plans to mess up my mission, and you're too pigheaded to realize that her plans are pathetic. Bombs? Seriously? Old Tomkins got me into the city through the east gates without even making the guards suspicious. That's the kind of stuff you can do when you've got a *real* Strategist."

I got hot when he insulted Erin. I clenched my fists and twisted away, mutinous thoughts flashing through my mind. I filled my lungs with air, feeling it gust sultrily into my chest, and breathed out slowly, trying to blunt my razor-sharp fury. No matter how much Breesten and I despised each other, we were on the same side – we had to penetrate the palace's defenses and kill the king. The most logical thing to do was work together.

"Listen, Tack," I said evenly, trying to sound friendly, "let's make a deal."

"I don't want any deal with you," Breesten said, assiduously refusing to look me in the face. "You're trying to take all the credit for yourself!" His voice had swelled in volume so much that I winced, eyes darting from side to side to make sure nobody was giving us suspicious glances.

"Shh, Tack," I pleaded in a whisper. "We're going to get caught if you keep yelling like this." I grabbed his sleeve and tried to yank him down the street as surreptitiously as possible.

We ducked behind a rusty fountain. An unimpressive trickle of water leaked from its spout, sending brown-tinted drops onto the street. It was large enough to hide the two of us from passing Zakarrans, but I kept my voice low as I said, "Tack, I know you can't stand me, but I need to help you kill the king."

He opened his mouth, but I pressed on before he could interject. "I don't care about the glory or the credit. You can have that. I just need to be sure that the deed is carried out."

He ran his fingers through his clumpy hair and said, "Why do you care about this so much? Why can't you let me accomplish my mission in peace?"

"Because I need to be sure that you actually accomplish it! This isn't just a chance to strut around boasting about how you got a mission before anyone else. Lives, or at least one life, depend on your success."

Now Breesten's eyes had lost their manic ire and were fixed on me in dawning realization. "So *that's* why Erin was screaming at me earlier," he said.

I felt a burst of impatience. "Erin never screamed at you, Breesten."

He shrugged. "Well, she told me I had better kill the king or her best friend might die." He slouched out of his antagonistic stance and said, "You're her best friend. She thinks that you're going to die."

I nodded.

Breesten snorted. "That's the most brainless thing I've ever heard."

I turned away from him, fuming. It was one thing for Breesten to poke fun at *me;* we'd been bickering continuously for years. But he had no right to insult Erin's intelligence. She was a hundred times smarter than him. She was a hundred times smarter than anyone I knew.

My fist was clenched so tightly at my side that I felt my fingers cramping and my knuckles popping out like hard bumps against my skin. I wanted nothing more than to punch Breesten's gorilla-ish face, but if I wanted to convince him to let me help with the mission, I knew I had to practice self-control.

"I don't need your help, Nichols," Breesten growled.

"Well, you're getting it anyway," I growled back. "No one will ever need to find out you had my help. All the glory will be yours."

Breesten's eyes had lost their smoky rage, and he appeared as thoughtful as I'd ever seen him. "I don't care about the glory," he said, but we both knew that was a lie. He'd spent his whole life clamoring for glory, competing against me in the fifty-meter dash on the playground as little kids, reveling in glee every time he scored higher than me on a test, always needing to be the best. I knew he loathed the fact that I was a Fighter. In Domina, Fighter was probably the most exalted and honorable of all professions, and Breesten's pride at becoming one was marred by the fact that I, his lifelong rival, had accomplished the same feat. "All right," said Breesten, "I'll let you tag along for now. But only because you'd try to mess everything up if I refused."

I still wanted to thump him, but at least now we were on the same team.

"Okay," I said. "We need to get into the palace. Does Tomkins have some brilliant plan for that?"

"Easy," said Breesten. "First, I've got to find some sort of back entrance, out of sight of the street."

"I found one," I told him. "But there's a guard."

"Perfect – show me."

I led him around the brightly decorated wall and pointed out the small door, which was protected by a single bored-looking sentinel. Breesten glowed with excitement as he reached beneath his long coat and pulled out a sleek sword.

I started to sweat. "What are you doing?"

"Getting into the palace."

I stared at the furbished blade, which shone like a wicked grin, eager and able to slice through human bodies without regard to the life contained inside. I shot a glance at the guard. He was only a little older than me, with a round, serious face and pants at least an inch too short for his legs. He had his own sword strapped to his side, but I doubted he could stand under Breesten's surprise attack.

"Tack, no –" I hissed.

"What's wrong with you?" Breesten asked. "Stay out of the way and watch how a true swordsman works."

He began to advance, but I jumped in front of him. "No! Wait!"

Breesten scowled fiercely. "I'm beginning to regret letting you come with me. Now get out of the way!"

Our raised voices had been enough to grab the attention of the guard, and he loped toward us now, looking relieved to have something to do. "Hey!" he called, "What are you two yelling about over there? Bring your argument away from the king's residence; if the sound of your yelling reaches His Majesty's ears, he won't be amused."

In half a blink, Breesten whirled, and his sword flew up to press against the poor guard's throat. The guard raised his hands hastily, trying not to swallow, eyes crossed as he kept them warily on the blade on his jugular. He hadn't even had time to reach his own weapon.

Breesten licked his lips and looked at the guard in the way a hungry wolf might look at a tender lamb. His fingers tightened on the hilt. "Your blood will be the first to stain my sword," he hissed, and the guard made a terrified squeaking noise. Breesten was breathing hard and grinning crazily as a drop of blood appeared on the blade. "You should feel honored."

"Tack – no – stop it!" Horror slopped through my veins like ice as I watched the crimson drop splatter onto the ground, leaving a smear on the asphalt. I grabbed his hand and tried to wrench it from the guard's throat, but Breesten shoved me impatiently away.

"I'm going to slit open your neck nice and slowly," he told the guard. "This is my first kill, and I want to relish the moment."

"Please, please…" the guard gurgled, sinking to his knees. Tears streamed down his cheeks and dripped onto the sword.

"Breesten! Stop!"

I knew it was his job – our job – to exterminate the enemy, to kill. But the sight of this whimpering man at Breesten's mercy wasn't the picture of glory I had expected. I hadn't thought that killing would be like this

– in fact, I'd never really considered the *killing* part of being a Fighter. Right now all I could think was that I was going to be sick.

Erin would know what to do, but Erin wasn't here and there was no time to text her. As Breesten's eyes flashed in anticipation of the guard's last gasp, I threw myself between the two and kicked Breesten's sword out of his hand. It clattered to the ground, and I grabbed it by the pommel and let it hang at my side.

"Linna!" Breesten snarled, hate etched into the scowling lines of his face. The guard put a hand to the thin cut beneath his chin, breathing laboriously, and staggered several steps backward.

"You can't kill him," I said firmly. Breesten lunged for his sword, but I dodged to the side and held it out of his reach.

"Then how are we supposed to get inside?" Breesten demanded. "You're the one who's going to die if we – if *I* – don't succeed. Maybe I should just let that happen!"

He turned furiously to the guard, who was massaging his throat. "Don't you dare tell anyone about this," he said threateningly. "If you do, a hundred Dominan Fighters will tear your limbs apart and torture your family. And you'd better let us into the palace, or you'll pay with your life."

"I can't!" the guard croaked, eyes wide with fear. He fixed his dilated pupils on me. "Please, tell him I can't!"

I advanced a step toward him, trying to twist my face into a hardhearted sneer. As much as I abhorred Breesten for his obsession with butchery, I needed to take on his personality for a moment in order to gain access into the palace. "If you tell anyone about this," I warned, "I'll make sure he finishes slitting your throat."

Sniveling pitifully, the guard bobbed his head up and down.

"Now let us in!" Breesten demanded, but before the guard could heave open the gate, the thunderous sound of a mob of footsteps echoed from a nearby alley.

"Tack!" I said, and pointed in the direction of the noise. He muttered a string of incomprehensible obscenities under his breath and then sprinted in the opposite direction. I flew after him, leaving the guard to stand alone in front of the gate, a mixture of tears and blood dampening the collar of his uniform.

We finally stopped for breath when we had run several blocks. My lungs stung from the surge of effort, and my heart drummed a million beats per second from an amalgamation of fear, anger, and physical exertion.

Breesten whirled on me. "See what you did!" he shouted. "I could be in the palace by now! King Gerald could be dead! But you slowed me down, and now we won't be able to get in through the back door because a circus will be trooping animals through it until late tonight!"

"Circus?" I said dumbly.

"You wouldn't know, since you don't have a real Strategist," Breesten snapped. "Tomkins found out that King Gerald has ordered a circus from a faraway continent to entertain him tonight for dinner."

I looked again at the ragged people and ancient cars swirling down the cracked street. If the king of Zakarra was rich enough to import circuses from distant lands for his own mealtime amusement, why couldn't he help his own subjects? I remembered what the redheaded boy had confided to me regarding King Gerald. *"I almost wish that someone* would *kill him. Know what I mean?"*

Now I thought that maybe I did know.

"It's okay," I told Breesten, trying to reassure myself as much as him. "We still have a whole day to carry out your mission."

"No, *I* have a whole day. Not *we*. It was a mistake to say you could help. From now on, this mission is completely *mine*." Breesten shot me one last contemptuous scowl and strode fuming down the street, overlong arms swinging angrily at his sides.

Also furious, I turned around and tried to navigate through the twisting Zakarran streets back to the alley where Erin had blown a hole in the wall, but all the streets looked the same. In Domina there were always majestic gardens or gushing fountains lining the streets to act as landmarks, but in Zakarra the buildings and houses looked like jumbled puzzle pieces, scattered along the roads in no particular order, indistinguishable from one another.

My texter buzzed in my pocket, making me jump, and I pulled it out hurriedly. Erin's message danced across the screen. *Linna, hurry up! We need to leave now to get back to Domina on time.*

I grimaced. If I didn't get home at the same time I would return from university, Dad would get suspicious. *I'm lost,* I typed to Erin.

You're hopeless, Erin typed back, which was not encouraging.

Trying to quell the tempestuous panic gusting in my chest and knocking my numb heart, I swallowed my emotions and forced myself to think. I looked around and saw a brick building hugging the curb. I remembered the fortuneteller backing me against a brick wall – feeling slightly more confident, I chose my direction and broke into a run.

Now that I knew approximately where I was, I started to recognize the streets as I dashed down them. My breaths and strides joined into a quick rhythm, and for a minute I enjoyed the whoosh of wind and sensation of speed. But then the fortuneteller's prediction thrummed through my head to the tempo of my footsteps in a relentless chant. *"You are doomed to die!"*

Thinking about death made me think about all the things I still wanted to do in my life, like run a marathon, or color the entire white marble front of my house with crayons, or help Erin blow up a car. I wanted to do something great; it seemed like cheating for death to snatch me before I'd even had a chance to accomplish anything.

Thinking about death made me think about my mom, who had died before my second birthday. I didn't remember anything about her. My dad had always refused to speak of her when I'd battered him with questions when I was younger, so I'd learned not to mention my mother. I didn't even know how she had died.

I realized now that I needed to know.

My thoughts had shoved awareness of my environment from my mind, but now I flew from my trance as a beefy man in a smart uniform stepped in front of me.

"Hold up a minute, young lady; what's your hurry?" he demanded. He had a sword at his side, and some sort of badge flashed in the sun on his hefty chest. I deduced he was a Zakarran policeman.

"No – no hurry," I panted, shrinking away. "I just like to run."

His eyes narrowed to a squint. "You have a strange accent," he said. "You're not from Zakarra." I tried to back away further, but he shortened the distance between us in two swift steps, hand on the hilt of his sword. "Did you know that a Dominan assassin is going to try to kill the king?"

I shook my head furiously. "I don't know anything about that," I babbled. "I'm not from Domina. I'm from… I'm from… the circus!"

"The circus that will be entertaining King Gerald tonight? But then why aren't you at the palace?" he asked distrustfully.

"I'm not a performer," I explained. "I just, you know, look after the animals. I give them food, make sure they have enough water… trim their nails and, um, make sure they sleep at night. Except for the nocturnal animals – those I make sure sleep during the day."

The policeman grunted, and I worried that he'd seen through my flimsy story. But then he stepped aside to let me pass. "Make sure you behave yourself, since I'm letting you roam Zakarra's streets," he said. "Circus people are quite mischievous, aren't they? I'd better not see any vandalism on my route tomorrow."

"Of course not," I breathed, hardly daring to believe my luck. "Thank you, sir."

I waited till he was halfway down the block before breaking into a sprint.

I ducked into an alley, followed its narrow, snakelike path, and found the dumpster at the end. I clambered over and spilled sloppily onto the ground on the other side.

Erin leapt from where she'd been sitting against the wall. "I got impatient and came here to wait for you – come on, we've got to hurry!" she urged, steering me to her car.

I followed, panting, and climbed into the passenger's seat. Erin twisted her key in the ignition, pressed her foot onto the accelerator, and shot out of the clump of trees in which the car had been hidden. As we bumped and rolled toward the road, I filled her in on what I'd learned.

"I think I can probably get into the palace tomorrow," I said. "The guard we pressured is pretty terrified of Breesten and me."

Erin nodded approvingly. "As long as he doesn't blab that two Dominan Fighters threatened him at the point of a sword."

Now doubts began to seep into my mind again. "Do you think that's likely?"

Erin shrugged. "I would suggest stuffing some money in your pocket tomorrow before you try to infiltrate the palace."

"Why?" I asked.

She grinned. "Bribery."

I opened my mouth to tell her that bribery was immoral, but then I remembered that murder was also immoral and closed it again. Erin hummed as she drove down the road at top speed, car swerving precariously to the left, then to the right. With a pang, I realized that driving with Erin was another thing I'd miss when I was dead.

I still didn't want to tell Erin about the fortuneteller's forecast. The knowledge sat uncomfortably in my head like a heavy weight I couldn't shake off. I'd never kept anything important from Erin before; we'd been such good friends for so long that I'd thought it was impossible for secrets to exist between us.

As if reading my mind, Erin asked, "How did you finally find the palace?"

"An old lady told me," I said. "I almost killed her."

The car swerved even more sharply. Erin yanked the wheel back into position and straightened out our course. "You? Almost kill an old lady?"

"It was a move my dad taught me a long time ago," I said, not meeting her eyes. "She grabbed me from behind. I thought she was trying to attack."

The car started zigzagging crazily, and I realized Erin was shaking with laughter. I grabbed the wheel to steady it, but she brushed my hand away. When I still hadn't joined her mirth a few moments later, Erin shot me a concerned look. I turned away and stared at the passing countryside, pretending to be very interested in the orange-leaved trees. I didn't feel like laughing. All I could think about was the fact that I was going to die.

~ 5 ~

Thanks to Erin's maniacal driving, we arrived back in Domina just as the students of Dexter University surged from campus after their last class of the day. I sagged with relief. We'd made it. My dad would never know that I had skipped school to go to Zakarra.

We veered into my driveway, and I slid from the car. The house was towering and familiar, but I didn't want to go inside; I wanted to sit in the passenger seat beside Erin as she drove forever and feel my stomach drop every time we bounced over a bump. But I knew that right now I had to face my dad.

"Can you pick me up really early tomorrow?" I said. "The way things went today, I'll probably need all day to even sneak into the palace, not to mention find King Gerald and kill him."

"Anything for you, my friend," said Erin brightly. I started to walk away, but she called me back. "Have you thought about how you're going to carry out the deed?"

A shiver tickled my spine like a cold, crawling spider. "What do you mean?"

"How are you going to kill the king?"

"Well… um…"

"I can loan you a bomb, if you like. Though that could be very loud and very messy."

I winced at the thought of King Gerald's body parts flying in all directions as an explosion ripped him apart. "No thanks. Breesten has a sword, and I think I'll... um... rely on my fists."

"A chop to the windpipe would be swift and silent," Erin suggested.

"Yeah, okay." Suddenly, I couldn't wait to get away. I'd practiced chops like the one Erin had proposed countless times before, but the thought of my hand crushing a living being's airway made me feel nauseous.

I hurried the rest of the way up the driveway and let myself in through the door Erin and I had recently repaired. My stomach grumbled stridently and I realized how starved I was; I hadn't eaten anything since my bowl of cereal at breakfast. I knew I should eat a lot tonight so I'd have energy to carry out whatever plan Erin invented for tomorrow.

I'd just dipped my fork into an enormous bowl of steaming noodles when the door thumped open and my dad grumped into the house, scuffing his shoes on the mat. The shadowy pits under his eyes were deeper than I'd ever seen them, dark like bottomless lunar craters against his white cheeks, and he looked like he hadn't combed his hair. The first thing he did was yell my name. "Linna!"

I jumped. "I'm here! What's wrong?" My fork clattered over the edge of my bowl and onto the table.

"You know very well what's wrong," Dad raged. "Tell me, why weren't you at university today?"

Shock slammed against me like a stinging slap. How could he know I wasn't at university? Erin had told me Phil Falconer had agreed to tell the professors I was sick. "I... I was there," I fibbed desperately, knowing it was hopeless.

"Don't lie to me," Dad said in a dangerous tone. "James – Professor Scurius to you – is my old friend; he called and asked if you were feeling better. When I admitted I didn't know what he was talking about, he told me that you hadn't shown up to class today because you were sick." He stomped to the table and slammed his briefcase down with a bang. "Or *pretending* to be sick."

I suddenly felt very small, and I guess the color must have drained from my face because Dad looked at me more closely and said, "You aren't really sick, are you?"

Truth to be told, I didn't feel too great at the moment, but I simply shook my head. "No," I whispered. "Not really."

He thumped a fist on the table with such force that my bowl vibrated and my fork clattered. "Then where were you, Linna? I have enough on my mind already without adding a truant to my worries!"

"I was – " I scourged my mind for an excuse. "I was trying to avoid Phil Falconer."

"Phil?" Dad raged. "That fool who beat you in the Fighter ranking test?"

I nodded. "I think… I think he's in love with me. That's what Erin said, anyway."

"Erin!" He fumed. "I should have known she had something to do with this! Did she skip school today as well? I suppose that she convinced you to play hooky!"

I shook my head frantically; I didn't want to impugn Erin, too. "No! It was all my idea. I forced her to skip class with me."

"Is that so?" He looked at me like he could see through my skin and nervous stance into my thoughts.

"So tell me, Linna, if you weren't at university, and you weren't at home, where were you all day?"

He saw me start. "Yes," said Dad, "I know you weren't in the house – I came home for an hour for lunch, and you weren't here. Then I came by again after Professor Scurius called me, and the house was still empty."

I felt like all my organs were sinking inside me as I struggled madly for excuses, but my mind stubbornly refused to produce any sort of explanation, plausible or otherwise. The only thing I could think was that I wished Erin was here. Erin excelled at concocting stories under pressure.

Dad took a step closer. *"Where were you?"*

"I'm not telling," I said quietly.

His jaw quivered like he was trying to smother his anger before it exploded. I experienced a flash of guilt – and then a sense of satisfaction. He may have had the power to sacrifice my life, but I could still make him furious. Suddenly, I was hot with anger; I was more enraged with him than I'd ever been in my life. I felt myself shaking.

"I am the *Governor,* Linna," Dad said. "I can't have my daughter fail to attend her classes and undermine my authority like a common rebellious teenager, especially since you are the first female Fighter in over a hundred years."

"What's that supposed to mean?" I snapped.

"It means everyone will be watching you. And truancy is unacceptable."

"You know what's unacceptable?" I seethed. "What's unacceptable is you…"

I was going to say that it was unacceptable for a father to sacrifice his child for public execution in an enemy city-state, even if he was the Governor. But my throat refused to sound the words, and they sputtered away as Dad's voice rose in a fresh wave of fury. *"Will you tell me where you were!"*

"No!"

"TELL ME!"

"NO!"

Dad took a deep breath and clenched his fists, just like I did whenever I was angry. Right now my nails were imprinting sharp half moons deep into my palms. Obviously struggling to control the volume of his voice, Dad said, "Linna, you've been acting very oddly since the Fighter ranking test two days ago – "

I gritted my teeth as though I could use them to restrain my feverishly beating heart.

"This is the last time I'm going to ask you," Dad said. "Where were you today when you were supposed to be at class?"

I saw his fist flexing at his side, big and hard like a knuckled hammer. Dad had been a Fighter when he was younger, before he became one of the triumvirate. For an instant, I grasped at the scrawny hope that he would understand how important it was that I didn't let Breesten mess up his mission, that I *fight* for my life instead of simply let it slip away.

"I was in Zakarra," I said, my words barely audible.

Dad jerked, and the table jumped as he knocked against it. "What did you say?" Now his voice was just as quiet as mine.

"I was in… the car," I said more loudly. "Erin's car. Hiding from Phil Falconer. We had a box of doughnuts, and we ate them all. Now are you happy?"

"No, I'm not!" Dad yelled. "Tomorrow you will go to all your classes and apologize to your professors. I never want you to skip university again, Linna; do you understand?"

"Yes, sir."

"Good!" He picked his briefcase back up and stomped upstairs, footsteps booming the way my imagination sounded gunshots in my nightmares. I exhaled slowly to calm myself. I'd told him I understood his order, but I had no intention of obeying.

I sat down again – I'd leapt to my feet during the argument – and forced down a mouthful of now tepid noodles. My throat felt stiff as I swallowed. It pained me to keep secrets from my father, but I knew I couldn't tell him about my clandestine visit to Zakarra. If he found out, he'd forbid me to go back, and I needed to go back to finish the mission in case Breesten failed.

Then the door swung open again. This time it was Erin who traipsed into the kitchen.

"Guess where I've been," she said. Without waiting for me to guess, she plowed on, "I snuck into Tomkins's office and found the file on Breesten's mission. It's been updated since yesterday. There was loads of information in there; I memorized the important parts." She scraped a chair across the linoleum floor to join me at the table.

I perked up, slurping a knot of noodles.

"Apparently, there are political tensions in Zakarra right now," Erin said. "King Gerald was a good king until about two years ago – but then I guess the power corrupted him, because since then he's been spending all his wealth on himself instead of on the people."

I remembered the ornate palace I'd seen in Zakarra and what Breesten had said about a circus coming to entertain the king, and then I recalled the beat-up vehicles, downcast people, and shabby buildings. I remembered the fortuneteller's soiled jacket and the way she'd snatched eagerly at my meager coin, grinning in pitiful anticipation of the scant meal it could buy. "Yeah," I said. "That makes sense."

"King Gerald isn't even *reasonably* immoral," said Erin. "I mean, if I ran a city-state, maybe once in awhile I'd use a bit of the tax money to buy an ice-cream cone or something, but King Gerald is extravagant. He has a pet emu, chefs to cook him gourmet meals every day, a swimming pool…"

"How's this going to help me kill him?" I interrupted.

Erin shrugged. "No idea, but at least you know whose windpipe you're going to crush. I thought it might make you feel better about killing him."

I was about to tell her that it did not make me feel any better when she pulled a two-way texter from her pocket. "Hold on," she said, "I have a message from Phil."

"What?" I shot her a befuddled expression.

"I had another pair of texters, so now I can communicate with both him and you."

"Why would you want to communicate with Phil Falconer?"

"In case something goes wrong while you're in Zakarra and I'm waiting outside the wall," she explained, eyes flicking over the text. "I thought it would be a good idea to have a lifeline back in Domina."

I didn't know how I felt about one of the world's most annoying people serving as my lifeline. "What does he say?" I asked.

Erin stuffed the texter back in her pocket. "He asks if there's anything else he can do to help."

I shook my head. "Tell him he already spoiled his first assignment – we're not giving him another." Then I debriefed Erin on how my dad knew I'd skipped school. "He says I have to be in class tomorrow, and I need to apologize to my professors."

"Surely you're not going to listen to him!"

I shook my head. "No, there'll be time for apologies after my life is no longer in jeopardy."

Erin grinned; she loved it when I broke rules.

Heavy footsteps approached the kitchen. I wiped the smile off my face and bent over my empty bowl as Dad entered the room.

"Hello, Governor Nichols!" Erin said, flashing him a charming smile.

"What are you doing here?" Dad demanded.

"Telling Linna that it was a bad idea to play hooky today and that we should apologize profusely to our professors tomorrow. Maybe even bake them cookies."

"OUT!" Dad roared, and I knew that he could tell she was lying.

"Goodbye, Governor Nichols!" Erin waved in farewell and hastily absconded, giving no clue that she'd noticed the glare that burned from my father's eyes.

As soon as Erin left, a tense silence descended on the house. I tried to crack it. "Dad, I'm sorry."

"That you skipped school and have spent your entire life being best friends with a hooligan?"

"Um…yeah. Sure. I'm sorry."

After a moment's hesitation, Dad said awkwardly, "I'm not perfect either, you know."

"Really?" I said, with just enough sarcasm that his eyebrows shot up, but not enough to make him say anything. I decided to take advantage of this rare lapse in his stern personality.

"Dad," I said, "I want to know about Mom." He stiffened, and I let the words tumble out, scared that if I didn't say them now, I'd never get another chance. "I want to know how she died."

The line of his lips tightened. "That's, um, a very painful memory for me to tell, Linna," he said.

I remembered what Erin had said about Dad and I being masochists. "Maybe pain is healthy sometimes," I said.

Dad breathed out noisily and gave a slow nod. "Maybe," he admitted. "But not always." I was startled to see that I could sense his mind churning inside his head, thinking that he didn't want to tell me anything, but knowing that he was obligated to tell me, because if he didn't and I died, he would never get to tell anyone.

"It was before I joined the triumvirate," he said softly. "I was still a Fighter, and you were just a toddler. Your mother was a battlefield nurse."

I nodded, encouraging him to continue.

"We were at the Battle of the Hills, me fighting and your mother tending the wounded, and everything seemed fine. I was fighting better than I'd ever fought before, probably because Kendria – your mom – was there, and I wanted to impress her. Whenever I had a chance to breathe, I'd glance at the medical tent and see her watching me. I'd struck down nearly a dozen men when I heard her yell. I didn't react – I was pulling my sword from an enemy's body – but then I saw her in my peripheral vision, sprinting through the battlefield. I turned around just in time to see her attack an enemy warrior directly behind me." He swallowed. "The warrior had his sword raised; he'd been about to stab me in the back. Your mom lunged at him to stop him from killing me, and he drove his sword into her instead."

I saw a drop of wetness glinting on his eyelid like a crystal in a ring.

Dad gasped as the memories hit him like excruciating blows. "And then I saw – her blood jumping out – and splashing on the ground." He swiped his eyes. "She was pregnant, you know. It was going to be a boy. You would have had a younger brother, and I would have had a son. We were going to name him Stirling."

I felt numb, like I'd been dipped in ice. "What did you do?" I asked. My tongue felt like it acted from far away, like it wasn't connected to the rest of me.

"I struck your mother's murderer with the hilt of my sword," Dad continued. "He crumpled to the ground. Then I felt an arm on my shoulder and knew that one of his comrades had come to his aid, so I used that special move I taught you and flipped him over my back so he landed in front of me. Then I ran my blade through his heart.

"The battle had seemed an even match till then, but suddenly I was so angry that I felt like I could stomp my foot and squash the world. I fought like I was invincible, until I was drenched in enemy blood. That night, I was the only parent who returned home to you. You didn't cry when I told you Mom wasn't coming back. You didn't understand."

I wasn't crying now either, but Dad was. Tears ran down his cheeks like lines of grief, and he didn't even look ashamed. My whole body throbbed with a sensation similar to fear; as far as I knew, Dad never cried; I'd never seen him show an emotion so openly.

"Kendria was perfect," he sniffled. "As perfect as a human being could be, anyway. She was smart and kind and made me laugh. She loved art. She was excellent at drawing, and she thought you might be too, when you got older. She bought you your first box of crayons."

Now I remembered laying on the floor of Dad's office when I was little, scribbling away in bright colors.

"But suddenly she was gone," Dad said, "and it was completely my fault. She'd died to save me, and I knew I'd never see her again. I didn't deserve to see her. But when you got older, I saw how much you were like her. Seeing Kendria reflected in you made me so…happy. And I knew I didn't deserve that happiness, not when I was to blame for her death. All I deserved was pain. So I tried to squash her out of you, to make you more like me."

I thought of all the times that he had told me to set aside my drawings so that he could give me a lesson on historic battles or various weapons. How whenever I complained about Tack Breesten's competitiveness, he'd urged me to outdo him, filling my mind with martial arts. "Did it work?" I asked.

Dad gazed at me for a few seconds, and I saw a deep sadness fill his eyes behind the tears. "I'm afraid it did," he said.

~ 6 ~

I didn't know what to feel or what to think. I watched Dad bury his face in his arms, and he stayed there for so long that he might have stopped breathing. I left him and wandered upstairs, hand dragging on the railing, and stepped into my room. I locked the door.

My bed looked like a yawn, long and welcoming sleep, so I lay down on top of my blankets and stared at the creases in my pillowcase. I hadn't known Mom had died in battle. I hadn't known anything about her except that she had dark hair like me, and I'd only discovered that from the few photographs of her I'd managed to find.

I reached beneath my mattress and pulled out one of those photographs now. Mom and Dad stood smiling in front of an elaborate, spraying fountain. Mom cradled me in her arms; I was bundled in a blanket so only my face showed. She looked happy. Her eyes were blue like mine and danced like the drops that rained from the fountain's spout.

I woke up the next morning feeling completely empty, except for a hard knot of dread that sat like a sour lump in my gut. I almost rolled over and went back to sleep, but then I remembered how I'd asked

Erin to pick me up early today. If I wanted to live, I needed to hurry up.

Dad was already eating breakfast by the time I reached the kitchen. He glanced at me briefly, but didn't give any sign that last night's conversation had occurred. I would've thought I'd imagined it except that the sadness stretching apart my insides felt painfully real.

A bang rang the door, and Dad jumped and spun around, but he relaxed when he realized it wasn't a bomb. Erin lowered her leg – she'd kicked the door open – and deposited the enormous plate in her hands on the table in front of my dad.

"Good morning, Governor Nichols," she said. "As I drove home last night, I couldn't help but think that I may have angered you yesterday, so I baked you these cookies to show that I am sincerely sorry and that I hope from now on, we will get along like cake and icing, minus the being eaten part."

She picked up a cookie from the plate and offered it to my dad. After a moment of hesitation, he took it and examined it closely.

"It's white chocolate chip," Erin said. "Your favorite."

Dad's eyebrows rose. "How did you know my favorite type of cookie?"

Erin smiled smugly. "I'm a Strategist. I know pretty much everything."

"I doubt even Perceval Tomkins knows my favorite type of cookie," Dad said, still staring at the treat in his hand like it was an astonishing anomaly.

"Well, I know many things that Professor Tomkins knows not. And that cookie is for eating, not aesthetic pleasure. Come on, Linna. Time to go."

"Wait," Dad said, "your first class doesn't begin until eight. There's no need to leave so early." He seemed to find our premature departure dubious, and I almost quailed under his frown, but Erin leapt to my rescue.

"I was going to buy Linna breakfast at Little Dagger Café before school," she said. "As an apology for convincing her to join me in truancy yesterday, which I now admit was a very bad idea."

"Aw, go ahead," said Dad, waving us out the door with the hand still holding the cookie. Before the door closed behind us, I glanced back to see him lift the cookie to his mouth and take a bite.

We flew to the car, and Erin celebrated our escape by speeding down the driveway, pulling an inexpert U-turn, and slamming her hand hard on the horn. It was barely light, the sun poking pink tendrils from its nest beneath the horizon to test the new day, and the sight was almost beautiful enough to fill me with hope that perhaps I might succeed. Perhaps I might actually kill King Gerald and live to taste tomorrow.

"You're amazing," I told Erin as she zoomed down the street, weaving between the slower-moving early morning cars. "Dad was irate at you last night, and you managed to get back on his good side just by bringing him cookies!"

"His favorite cookies," said Erin.

"How did you know they were his favorite?"

"Easy. He obviously doesn't like chocolate, because chocolate contains endorphins that produce a feeling of happiness and well being, and as he never seems very happy, I deduced that he does not consume an adequate amount of cocoa. So then I asked myself, if a man refused to eat chocolate, what would be his next best option? The obvious answer: white chocolate. Since chocolate chip cookies are the childhood favorite of most people, I figured that your dad was most likely to be partial to white chocolate chip cookies on the rare occasions when he could find them."

For the millionth time in my life, I found myself awed by Erin's intelligence. "I didn't even know Dad's favorite kind of cookie," I said. Come to think of it, there were a myriad of things I didn't know, and if I died today I'd never get a chance to learn them.

Nearly twenty-five kilometers later, the car rolled over the top of a hill and Zakarra tumbled into view, nestled in its protective wall surrounded by autumn-colored trees. This time, I was ready for it when Erin swerved off the road and started crashing through the woods.

We hid the car in the same place as last time. I glanced at my watch impatiently as we set off on our hike toward the city-state's wall; every second spent romping through the woods was a second I could be spending trying to get into the palace. I wanted to take off for Zakarra at a full sprint, but I knew I couldn't leave Erin behind. I needed her; she hadn't told me the plan yet. And even more than her skills as a Strategist, I needed her with me as a friend for moral support.

Suddenly, my neck prickled. I spun around, shoes cracking on dry leaves, but I didn't see anything unordinary.

"What's wrong?" Erin asked.

I shook my head, trying to dislodge the feeling of unease. "Nothing. I just… I just had a weird feeling."

"Probably nothing," Erin assured me, and I nodded in agreement, but I still wasn't convinced.

The wall was only a minute's walk away now, and with every step my discomfort grew. For the first time, I wished I had a sword. I wanted to get away from here. "Let's hurry," I told Erin, and broke into a run.

"Stop!" Erin yelled, diving forward and grabbing my leg. I stumbled, fell forward, and caught myself on my hands to keep from landing face first on the mucky forest floor. "Turn around!" Erin shouted. "Run!"

I looked up to see a figure crashing through the woods straight toward us, sword in hand. I rocketed to my feet and shot off after Erin, glimpsing at least half a dozen more pursuers in my peripheral vision. I dodged a low-hanging branch and jumped a protruding root, trying to hear if the figures were gaining, but I couldn't hear anything beyond my flying feet and the frantic pulse throbbing in my ears, heavy with adrenaline. I drew alongside Erin.

I heard a grunt behind me, and the air whistled as something sharp cut through it. "Duck!" I grabbed Erin and yanked her head down. A sword twirled through the air over her head, brushing flying strands of bright red hair, and disappeared through the branches of a tree ahead of us, sending down a flurry of orange leaves like shards of broken glass.

I veered sharply right, Erin at my heels. I could hear shouts behind us, but now they grew fainter. I slowed down, and Erin dropped to a walk, panting. "You saved me from possible decapitation," she said.

"They tried to kill us!" I cried.

"Well, you're trying to kill their king," said Erin reasonably.

"Yeah, but why were they there? How did they know we'd come through the woods?"

"They probably found the hole I blew in the wall," said Erin. "They figured a Dominan assassin used it to get in yesterday and would most likely come back today to accomplish the deed, so they guarded it to stop the assassin."

"They could've caught us, but they stopped," I said. "Why did they stop?"

"Probably thought we were a decoy," said Erin. "Think about it – we're two weaponless girls, barely past the threshold of adulthood – neither of us look like probable killers. They must have thought we were sent ahead to lead them away from the opening. They didn't want to leave their post in case the real assassin slipped through the wall while they were away."

"Well, even if they were wrong, they accomplished what they wanted," I said. "Now we don't have a way into the city-state."

We broke into the clearing where we'd left the car. I hoisted myself through the passenger door, and Erin slid behind the wheel. "Don't be preposterous," Erin said. "There's still the gate." With a roar the engine burst to life, and we flew through the forest, dodging tree trunks and listening to dry branches scratch and drag along the roof and sides of the car.

As the car burst onto the road, I shuddered at the memory of the deadly sword flying over Erin's head, slicing the air in the exact space where her head had been a split second before. The thought that I had nearly just lost my best friend made me queasy. I wondered what it was like for her, knowing that if Breesten and I both failed the mission, her best friend would die. I snuck a glance at her as her fingers tapped the steering wheel. She looked calm but slightly strained, quieter than usual.

"Now would be a good time to tell me the plan for once I get in Zakarra," I said.

"Okay," said Erin. "Here's what I came up with: find the guard you saved from Breesten yesterday and tell him to let you into the palace. Say that if he refuses or raises an alarm, you'll kill him. Once you're inside, find the king's bedchamber – I assume he'd be in his bedchamber because he's been ill the last few years – break past any guards outside his door, barge in, and bash his head."

I wrinkled my nose.

"Try not to think about the grisly details too much," Erin advised.

"Do you think it's likely there will be guards outside his door?" I asked. "I don't know how I'll get past them."

"You'll figure it out; I know you will," said Erin, voice suddenly higher than normal. "You have to, Linna. If you don't, I'll blow up your bed and you'll have to sleep on the floor until I relent and get you a new one."

She noticeably avoided the fact that if I didn't figure out how to get past the guards, I wouldn't need my bed anymore.

"Is that the whole plan?" I asked.

"The main idea," said Erin. "Text me as you go, and I'll help you get by any obstacles you might face. Oh, and one more thing – if for some reason you find yourself on the roof of the palace in a life or death situation, jump off the east side."

Before I could ask Erin why she wanted me to commit suicide, she hit the brakes so hard that I would have flown through the windshield had my seatbelt not sliced against my shoulder, holding me to the seat. I turned my attention outside the vehicle and saw the road barred by Zakarra's massive gates. Four armed guards blocked the gates, looking warily at the car. Erin flashed them a cheerful smile through the window, then turned to me. "You need to get through the gates."

"I know – but I'll never convince the guards to open them."

Erin ignored me, squinting out the window, thoroughly studying each guard in turn. Then she grinned and turned back to me. "Don't worry," she said, "I have a brilliant plan."

She twitched her head at one of the guards. He had a bristly red beard and leaned casually against the wall, fingering his sword as he watched our car. "See that guy?"

"Yeah, he looks mean."

"Well, I don't think he's as mean as he appears. All you need to do is get out of the car, walk confidently up to him, and tell him that it has been a long journey, but the satisfaction of arrival is worth the grueling drive; you look forward to seeing him at dinner tonight."

"That's ridiculous," I protested. "He's just going to ask who in the world I am, and then he's going to run his sword through me!"

"You're only half right," Erin said. "He *is* going to ask who in the world you are, but he's not going to kill you, because you'll have an answer."

"And what is this answer?"

"You'll tell him that your name is Crystal, and you have journeyed for days from a distant city-state to meet your Aunt Ruby and her handsome husband." She caught my puzzled expression. "The handsome husband is the guard, in case you didn't get that part."

"How do you know his wife's name is Ruby? How do you know he even has a wife?"

Erin jerked her head again. "He has a ring on his finger, so he's obviously married. But the stone in the ring is red, an unusual choice for a wedding ring, and he has a tattoo on his forearm. If you look closely you can see that the tattoo is of the letter R enclosed in a heart. *Of course* his wife's name is Ruby! Seriously, Linna, don't you have eyes?"

"So his wife's supposed to be my aunt?" I said. "Wouldn't he know if his wife had a niece?"

"He thinks he would," said Erin wisely, "so it will come as a shock to him when he finds out his wife never mentioned her sister, Opal, or her sister's daughter, Crystal. But he loves his wife so much that he will look past her overlooking such a detail and open the gate for you."

"This'll never work," I groaned.

Erin looked insulted. "Come on, trust me."

I didn't want to put my faith into such a flimsy plan, but I didn't have much choice. Sure I would soon experience a sword through my heart, I climbed from the car and approached the red-bearded guard.

He watched, stony-faced, as I approached, and I was uncomfortably cognizant that the other guards traced my every move with narrowed eyes, hands on the hilts of their swords. I stopped in front of the red-bearded guard and looked up at him. He was tall and powerfully built; he could smash a fist on my head and flatten me to the ground if he wanted. I realized I'd already failed the first step of Erin's plan. She'd said to walk up to him *confidently*, and I didn't feel bold at all. I felt like I'd rather be anywhere in the world than here.

"Hi," I said, trying to keep my voice from cracking with fear.

"What is your business here?" the guard growled, beard jumping as he spoke.

"It has been a long journey, but now that I've arrived, I can look back and see that the drive was worth it," I recited. "I look forward to seeing you at dinner tonight."

His bushy eyebrows popped to the top of his forehead. "Would you like to explain who you are?" he asked.

No, I thought, but I bravely swallowed and said, "My name's Crystal, and I've come from a distant city-state to meet my Aunt Ruby – " At this his eyebrows bounced even higher – "and her husband." He looked perplexed, so I said, "You. You're her husband."

"Are you trying to tell me that you're my *niece?*"

"Um, yeah, I guess so."

Kill me quickly, please. Kill me quickly so I won't live long enough to hear Erin explaining how her plan would've worked if I hadn't messed it up as I choke my final breath.

The guard looked hesitant, uncertain whether he should cut out my insides or let me pass. "My mom's name is Opal," I blurted helpfully. "She wanted me to meet my Aunt Ruby. That was – that was her dying wish."

The guard's hand had been on the handle of his sword, but now he separated it from his weapon and held it out formally. "Good to meet you, Crystal," he said. "Welcome to Zakarra."

I shook his hand as relief flooded through me. Immediately, the other three guards started pulling open the heavy gates, and it took all my willpower to abstain from breaking into a run as I entered the city-state. Behind me, I heard the other guards questioning the red-bearded one.

"I didn't know you had a niece, Ronald."

"Ruby had a sister named Opal? I didn't know that; I thought she was an only child."

"Ronald, why didn't you tell us your sister-in-law had died?"

I peered over my shoulder in time to see Erin raise a hand in a mix of congratulations and farewell, and then her car roared crazily away down the road. I patted the texter in my pocket, making sure it was still there, and started jogging toward the palace.

Yesterday it had taken a long time to find the palace, but today I knew which direction to go. Past the narrow, shabby street where I'd asked the young boy for directions, past the brick wall where I'd encountered the creepy fortuneteller... My arrival in front of the palace walls came far sooner than I'd anticipated. I scanned the area, expecting a horde of guards to run at me with swords raised, but no one even glanced in my direction.

Now I somehow needed to sneak inside. The guard Breesten had intimidated yesterday was nowhere to be seen. My stomach ached from a combination of nervousness and hunger; I realized that I had never gotten a chance to eat breakfast. Maybe before I tried to assassinate the king, I should find something to eat.

Although breakfast seemed like a waste of time, it would be pointless to try and carry out Breesten's mission on an empty stomach. I strolled down the street, searching for a restaurant where I could buy something inconspicuously. Many early-rising Zakarrans darted in and out of buildings. Some held Styrofoam cups of coffee or doughnuts; others carried disposable dishes overflowing with scrambled eggs, sausages, and buttery biscuits.

"Where are you going?" a man in a faded green suit barked at me as I passed. "Loitering is not permitted, especially in the present circumstances."

"What present circumstances?" I asked, careful to imitate his accent.

"Someone's going to murder the king!" he explained. "Don't you know anything?"

I shrugged, deciding it was better to let him assume I was ignorant than to expose that I was the assassin.

"If you're going into the restaurant, do it quickly and clear out of the area," he ordered. "It's best not to complicate the guards' jobs any further."

I nodded and ducked into the nearest building. The saccharine scent of hot chocolate overwhelmed my senses and caused my insides to dance in longing. I stepped into a scraggly line of waiting customers and pulled some money from my pocket. My fingers brushed against Erin's texter, which buzzed against my skin.

I pulled it out and read her message. *Are you in?*

Yes, I replied. *I'm buying breakfast.*

Good, she answered. *Breesten just got into the city a moment ago. Maybe you should try and meet up with him.*

Maybe, I typed back. I doubted that Breesten would allow me to accompany him after our disagreement yesterday. For a moment I allowed myself to hope that he would carry out the king's murder without my assistance; that way I wouldn't have to perform the grisly deed myself. But then I forced myself to remain cynical. Until the king was declared good and dead, I needed to do everything in my power to eradicate him.

I stowed away the texter and handed the bored-looking woman at the counter a small cluster of coins. "Hot chocolate, please," I said. "And some waffles with bacon."

She narrowed her eyes, and I realized with a sinking feeling in my gut that I'd forgotten to disguise my accent. "Where are you from?" she asked. "I don't recognize you."

"I'm not from Zakarra," I explained hastily. "I'm visiting my aunt and uncle here."

She nodded and dumped my money into a cash register, but her expression remained suspicious as she poured a mug of steaming cocoa and shoved a plate across the counter. I ignored her, choosing instead to focus on my food. Having a satisfied stomach filled me with optimism; how hard could it be to kill a king? Erin had said herself that he was old and ill, and I was a Fighter of the most powerful city-state in the area. The odds were on my side.

I lifted my gaze from the heaping plate and watched the Zakarran citizens consume their meals. They seemed much happier in here, enjoying their meals, than they had scurrying through the streets. My eyes lingered on a familiar-looking young man with a boyish face and a thin red scar on his neck. With a start, I realized that it was the guard that Breesten had nearly killed yesterday.

He hadn't noticed me yet. I reached with fumbling fingers into my pocket and grasped the texter. My hands shook slightly as I tapped out a new message. *The guard we threatened is sitting at the next table. What should I do?*

As I waited for her reply, I angled my body so that the guard couldn't see my face. He appeared much more relaxed than he had the day before; his smart uniform had vanished, replaced by slacks and a striped shirt, and he was digging into a mound of sausages with obvious gusto.

The texter buzzed in my palm, and I glanced down to see Erin's reply. *Sit down across from him and force him to help you. He owes you.*

The young guard sat at a table by himself, staring at his plate as he shoveled sausage after sausage into his mouth. I picked up my plate and mug and casually slid into the chair across from him. He looked up and jumped in his seat, sending sausage grease dribbling down his chin. "You!" he sputtered.

"Shh!" I warned. "Keep it down." I looked over both shoulders to make sure no one had noticed his outburst, but thankfully the other customers seemed just as absorbed in their breakfasts as before.

The guard slammed down his fork, and when he spoke, his voice was a hiss. "You almost killed me!"

"No, I saved your life."

"But you were with him! You were with that guy with the sword who almost cut my head off – "

I swallowed a gulp of hot chocolate before cutting him off. "I know what happened," I said. "Listen, you need to help me get into the palace."

"I can't do that," he protested. "I don't have duty until noon, and I'd lose my job if I got caught."

"I think you *can* help me," I said, trying to adopt the smooth words and imposing tone Erin would use. "Because if you don't, I'll kill you."

His eyes swept up and down, sizing me up. He didn't seem impressed; his lanky frame probably would've towered eight or nine inches over mine had we stood, and it was obvious I had nowhere to conceal a weapon. "You couldn't kill me," he scoffed. "You don't even have a sword."

I leaned close to him and lowered my voice to a whisper, making sure the diners at neighboring tables couldn't hear. "I'm a Dominan Fighter," I said. "I'm in Zakarra to assassinate King Gerald. I don't *need* a weapon; the Governor of Domina gave me my first martial arts lesson before I knew how to read."

The terror that flickered across the guard's face was enough to raise a sharp stab of guilt in the back of my throat, almost choking me as I gulped a bite of waffle.

"I'll help you," said the guard. "But only because I'm too young to die, and because, in my opinion, King Gerald deserves to be killed as soon as possible." Then he slapped his hand over his mouth like he couldn't believe what he'd just said. "Don't tell anyone I said that," he said.

"I won't," I promised. I drained my last dregs of hot chocolate and got to my feet. "Can I meet you at noon at the back entrance to the palace?"

The guard nodded.

"Thanks," I said, and started to leave. But then I turned around. "What's your name, by the way?"

"Gordon," he said. "What's yours?"

I hesitated, wondering if it was wise to tell him my real name, but no pseudonyms popped into my head, so I said, "Linna."

He nodded, face showing the new respect that had appeared after he'd learned I was a Dominan Fighter. "Okay, see you at noon, Linna."

I slipped from the restaurant and bustled down the street, trying to look like I had a destination. If I was meeting Gordon at noon, I had a couple hours to kill. I felt disgusted at myself for threatening Gordon to force him to help me; he seemed like a nice guy, not any different than a normal youth in Domina. He seemed like the kind of person whom I might choose as a friend had we met under different circumstances.

The thought of friends reminded me that I needed to inform Erin of this new development. I ducked into the narrow alley between two ivy-covered buildings and tapped her a message on the texter, telling her that the guard would let me into the palace at noon.

Good work, she typed back. *Just make sure he doesn't blab.*

Don't worry. I threatened him with death.

But somehow I knew that I didn't need to worry about Gordon giving me away. I remembered the way he'd trembled and blubbered yesterday with Breesten's sword at his throat. He wasn't brave at all. He was just an overgrown kid who felt like he'd reached adulthood too early, sort of like me. I knew he'd do whatever I told him if it gave him the chance to preserve his life.

I navigated down a busy road, wanting to keep moving. Vendors lined the streets, their tables jammed with food and goods like tattered clothes and dog-eared paperback books, umbrellas propped over their heads to keep off the sun. Though when I glanced at the sky, I saw that the sun had retreated behind a layer of heavy gray clouds. I hoped the rain would hold off at least until the mission was complete.

I stopped at one table and thumbed through a faded book, pretending to be interested. Beside me, a lady in a smart coat negotiated with the grandmotherly woman manning the stand.

"This much for such a beat-up copy? That's outrageous, Elsie."

"Beat-up? You've got to be joking. It's practically new. And don't pretend you're wrung out on money, Mellie. I know you've got a good job as secretary for Head Advisor Piardak."

"Look, the pages are falling out and the cover's almost torn off. I'll pay half the price you're asking, but no more."

"Oh, fine then," said the old woman with a huff. The buyer – Mellie – passed some coins across the counter, and Elsie examined them one by one before dropping them in her change purse. But then she froze, one coin raised before her squinted eye.

"What's wrong?" asked Mellie.

"This coin isn't Zakarran," said Elsie. "It's the same size and shape and color, but instead of *Zakarra,* the engraving reads *Domina.* Wasn't someone from Domina going to try to kill the king?"

I fumbled with the book and took a step back. I wanted to fling down the paperback and sprint away, but that would only arouse suspicion. It was better to stay still and pretend I hadn't heard, to keep leafing through the book and try not to call attention to myself.

"Where did you get this coin?" the book vendor demanded.

"Now, Elsie, surely you're not accusing me of having anything to do with homicidal Dominan riffraff?"

"Of course not – I've known you for years, and I know you're too loyal to your city-state to be involved in any plots to kill King Gerald. But do you remember where this coin came from?"

"Yes, actually. An old woman gave it to me last night, begging for my bread crusts. She was completely loopy, said she was a fortuneteller. But you'd think that

Domina has enough lethal Fighters that its Governor wouldn't need to hire frail old ladies as assassins."

"Never mind that; we should bring the coin to the authorities. It proves that a Dominan has breached our walls!"

Consciously laboring to control my breathing, I set the book back on the table and hurried away at a fast walk. How could I have been thoughtless enough not to realize that Dominan coins would give me away? If a Zakarran policeman found the fortuneteller, she'd easily be able to describe me, and I could be caught. I'd also paid for my breakfast at the restaurant in Dominan coins; it was only a matter of time until someone opened the cash register and discovered the unfamiliar currency.

I ducked around a building and paced back and forth between a splintery planter of flaccid flowers and a concrete wall, listening to the noises of Zakarrans going about their lives on the other side of the building. I checked my watch, even though I knew it was too early to head for the palace. I didn't want a leery guard to catch me skulking around the king's dwelling, especially now that the authorities would know that a Dominan intent on killing King Gerald had gotten inside the city-state.

I turned a corner around the wall, intending to find a place closer to the palace to wait, and almost crashed into another figure as he hurried around the bend.

He yelped in surprise and drew his sword.

I looked up into the startled face of Tack Breesten.

~ 7 ~

"Oh, it's you, Linna." Breesten released a whooshing sigh of relief and stowed his sword back under his jacket. Then his forehead creased with anger. "I told you not to come back to Zakarra!"

I brushed off his disapproving words. "Tack, you have to be careful. People know that a Dominan is in the city, and they're going to be even more vigilant toward suspicious strangers lurking near the palace."

Breesten creased his forehead. "How do they know? Tomkins and I…" His voice trailed off. "You alerted them, didn't you?"

I chose not to answer. Breesten placed his hands on his hips as though his question had been confirmed. "I *knew* you'd mess it up! Why couldn't you just stay home like I told you?"

I lifted my chin defiantly. "Because you're too arrogant to realize that you need help. I doubt you've even found a way to get into the palace."

"Of course I haven't!" he snapped. "It's swarming with guards. I'm waiting for a chance to jump them and plow my way in by force."

I smiled smugly. "That's a terrible plan."

Breesten kicked a pebble at me. It skittered across the cracked asphalt ground, hit a bump, and flew into the side of the concrete wall. "Well, if you have a better idea, I'm open to suggestions," he said sarcastically.

"Actually, I *do* have a better plan," I said. I took my time telling Breesten about Gordon's agreement to let us into the palace at noon, relishing the sweet sensation of being in control, knowing what to do. This was probably how Erin felt all the time. No wonder she always seemed so happy.

I could see Breesten's mind churning behind his narrowed eyes. His fingers crept under his jacket and tapped his sword's pommel contemplatively, and I prayed he wouldn't decide to whip out his weapon and dispose of me before I could complicate his mission any further. But then he nodded, seeming to concede that my plan was a good one. "Okay," he said. "I'll go along with this. But I have one condition – I want to be the one to kill King Gerald. If you try to stop me, to stand in my way and try to claim all the glory for yourself, I'll kill you without hesitation to get to the king."

"Agreed," I said, inwardly relieved that I wouldn't have to perform the gruesome deed.

Breesten rolled up his sleeve to check his watch and grunted in impatience when he realized we still had well over an hour until twelve o'clock. I sat down on one side of the rough wooden planter, and he edged away to sit on the other side. I sent a quick text to Erin. *Found Breesten. He's coming with me at noon.*

Her reply made me grin. *I'm sorry. Maybe he'll fall on his sword after the murder so we won't have to listen to his boasting.*

Oblivious to my silent conversation, Breesten pulled out his sword again and started polishing it with a small cloth until it gleamed clean enough for him to see his reflection in the blade. I didn't know why he'd want to stare at his gorilla-like face, but at least furbishing his sword took his attention away from dialogue. I definitely wasn't in the mood to talk to him.

The minutes ticked by, and Breesten's sword now shone like a beam of light sharp enough to cut through flesh. Finally, he gave it a last, loving rub and stuck it back in its hidden hilt. He looked up to catch me watching.

"What's wrong?" he taunted. "Jealous that I have a sword and you don't? If you ever get a real mission – which I doubt you will, since you're number fifty-one – or prove extremely skilled in training, maybe you'll get one of these."

"I don't care about the sword," I seethed.

"Oh yes, you do. I know what you're like, Linna. You've always wanted to be better than me, ever since we were little and I teased you because I was taller than you. You got mad and learned how to read first, and you thought you were so smart until we raced the fifty-meter dash on the playground and I beat you."

"You beat me that one time," I protested. "I was faster every time after that."

"Yeah, until I turned thirteen, hit my growth spurt, and started training seriously to become a Fighter," said Breesten. "Now look at us. I'm the best new Fighter in Domina, and you're only number fifty-one."

Fresh fury surged inside me as I remembered the way Phil Falconer had cheated. Why did Breesten always have to be so competitive, even now, when my life might last only a few more hours?

"At least I have a real friend," I said defensively. "Falconer just follows you around like an infatuated puppy. He's only obsessed with you because you're Fighter number one."

Breesten snorted and turned away from me, hand on his belt above his sword. "You don't know anything, Linna." He looked at me over his shoulder and said, "Just because your dad is the Governor, it doesn't mean you're better than everyone else."

His words stung nearly as badly as being pricked by a sword. "That has nothing to do with our conversation!" I protested. "It has nothing to do with *anything!*"

He kept his back turned toward me so that all I could see were the three clumps of hair sticking up from his head. "You think you're so clever, sneaking into Zakarra to try to *assist* me on my mission." From the way he emphasized the word *assist,* it was obvious that he didn't expect me to be any help at all. "If you get in trouble, you'll just run crying to your father, Governor Nichols. He'll make sure that there aren't any consequences for your foolishness. He'll see to it that you get to do whatever you want, even if it involves sneaking into an enemy city to thwart a crucial Fighter mission."

"That's not true!" I argued. My dad would never stand up for me like that; he would more likely lock me up in the Dominan prison and disown me. He had no sympathy for me; if we didn't murder the king, he was going to ensure that I was *killed!*

I didn't want to hide here anymore, especially with Breesten raging at me. I lurched from the planter and stalked toward the corner.

"Hey, where're you going?" Breesten demanded.

"Away from you," I shot angrily, and broke into a run.

I bolted around the concrete wall and spilled back onto the busy street. No one looked at me twice as I dodged and weaved around passing people on foot or in slow-moving cars. A boy on a bicycle, boxes of fruits stacked high on the rack over his back wheel, braked suddenly to avoid hitting me and spat an expletive when his load of apples and tomatoes rolled in their containers.

"Linna! Hey!" The coarse yells plus a quick glance over my shoulder told me that Breesten was right behind me.

I ducked into a doorway and whirled around to face him. "What do you want?"

"I know what you're doing," said Breesten. "You're trying to ruin my mission. You're going to the Zakarran authorities to turn me in, because you can't stand the thought of me succeeding at something." He raised his left hand and wiped sweat from his eyes, which were manic and blazing from the run. "I can't let you do that," he said, and pulled out his sword.

"No! I'm not – " I started, but before I could say anything, Breesten made a jab.

His lunging sword rushed at my stomach, and I just managed to twist to avoid it. Breesten staggered forward, caught off balance, and the tip of his sword stuck in the wood of the door behind me. With a violent wrench, he yanked it free. I took advantage of the split-second diversion and ducked under his arm, tearing back down the street.

Breesten fumbled a moment before taking chase, heaving his sword back under his jacket so the Zakarrans on the road wouldn't see, and then exploded after me.

My legs flew and the wind tugged my gasping mouth, ripping my breath away. I knew I couldn't stay ahead of Breesten for long. I needed a place to hide.

I was in shock. I knew Tack Breesten and I had never gotten along, but I'd never imagined he'd try to *kill* me.

Suddenly, someone jumped in front of me, and I braked into a defensive stance. I quickly lowered my fists when I realized it was a Zakarran policeman. I tried to slide around him, heart thumping and eyes darting to glance behind me, wondering when Breesten would arrive, but the policeman put out his arm. "Why are you running?" he asked suspiciously.

In the present circumstance, I decided the truth would be my best option. "A guy with a sword's chasing me!" I panted.

The man's eyes widened. "Domina," he breathed.

And then I looked back to see Breesten hurling down the street toward me. I dodged around the policeman and fled, glancing back over my shoulder to see Breesten thump him in the temple with his elbow.

The policeman's eyes rolled back and he slumped still.

Breesten charged at me, leaping over the unconscious guard and trying to grab me by my ponytail, but I shot away and his hand clenched empty air. I sensed his ragged breathing behind me, rapid footsteps gaining. I whipped around a corner and heard him stagger to switch directions unexpectedly.

"Linna!" he yelled, his momentum slamming him into a wall. He bounced off and resumed the chase.

My throat and lungs burned. My legs were growing rubbery from running; I needed a break. Was it too early to meet Gordon at the back entrance? It was still before noon, but I couldn't think of anywhere else to go. My mind didn't seem to be working very clearly at the moment – panic had shoved every thought aside except for the knowledge that I needed to escape Breesten.

I cut between two buildings and took a sharp right. The palace loomed ahead of me, daunting walls casting short shadows. I tore around a cluster of women carrying groceries, and they stared after me in alarm. Despite my best efforts, my legs slowed stubbornly. I whipped around a corner onto a quiet street and spotted the back entrance; mustering my fear and transferring it into energy, I ran at it. My ears picked up the raspy sound of Breesten's breathing. He was gaining.

The texter bounced in my pocket, but I didn't dare reach down to pull it out. I wanted nothing more than to ask Erin what to do, have her tell me where to hide, but she wasn't here. Even if she thought she knew everything, there was no way she could know that Breesten was trying to kill me.

Breesten thundered less than a yard behind me. His shadow fell over my shoulder, chased by his hot breath. He grabbed my jacket, and I almost fell as he yanked me to a halt.

I looked a hundred meters down the street for the man guarding the back entrance, but he was looking the other way, fiddling with what seemed to be a loose thread on his sleeve. I couldn't call out. I couldn't alert the guard that Dominans had reached the palace.

Breesten reached beneath his jacket for his sword.

"Wait!" I stammered. "I don't want to turn you in! I don't want to ruin your mission!"

"Yeah, right," Breesten sneered, but his hand hesitated on the hilt.

"I want to help you," I insisted.

Then the texter in my pocket buzzed.

I thrust my hand into my pocket and pulled it out, keeping a wary eye on Breesten. His fingers were still wrapped around his sword, but he made no move to attack. I held up the tiny screen close to my face to read Erin's message.

It's almost noon. Make sure you're at the palace on time, if Breesten hasn't killed you yet.

I gritted my teeth and my fingers blurred as I hastily tapped out a response. *We're outside the walls. Breesten has drawn his sword and is preparing to murder me.*

Erin's reply appeared. *Tell him if he lets you live, I'll bake him cookies.*

I knew that was ridiculous, but trapped in Breesten's grasp with his sword leveled at my neck, I couldn't think of anything else to say. "Erin says that if you let me live, she'll bake you cookies!" I raised my arms protectively over my face and braced myself for death.

Breesten swelled with anger. "I don't care what Erin says! She's not even a real Strategist!"

The texter buzzed again in my hand, and I scanned the screen with frantic eyes. "Erin says that if you kill me, you will never get any honor for your mission, because killing the Governor's daughter is worse than failing to kill the king!"

Breesten looked like someone had just slapped him awake. He put his sword away and released his hold on my jacket. "I... I'm sorry, Linna," he said. "Please, don't tell anyone about this."

I inched away from him, livid and still shaking. I wanted to say that I'd tell everyone I knew he'd tried to kill me so they'd know what a monster he was, but this was the first time he'd ever begged me for anything. This was the first time I'd ever heard him say please.

And if we wanted a chance of killing the king, I needed him on my good side.

"Okay," I said, trying to slow my racing heart. "I won't tell anyone, but there are a few conditions that must be kept on your part."

"What sort of conditions?" he asked distrustfully.

"Well, you need to quit saying that I'm going to mess up your mission, you need to consider my ideas instead of just discarding them as hopeless, and you need to stop criticizing Erin."

Breesten scrunched up his face, making him look more like a gorilla than ever. "Okay," he said, and I could tell he loathed the word as it dropped off his tongue.

~ 8 ~

The guard still hadn't glanced in our direction, but I didn't want to make him wary by dallying within view of his post. I motioned to Breesten to follow me, then hurried to a rusty trash bin against the bright mosaic wall and crouched behind it, out of sight of the guard. Breesten dropped to his knees beside me, jerking up his sleeve to consult his watch. "Less than fifteen minutes till noon," he said.

I leaned against the wall and nodded wordlessly. My stomach heaved with nerves. As soon as Gordon let us in, navigating the palace undetected would be a matter of life or death. I had no idea what to expect once within the palace's walls.

Breesten chewed his gum loudly, each smack sending a throb through my skull. I wanted to tell him to cut it out, but I didn't want him to skewer me with his sword. I still couldn't believe he'd tried to kill me. Even if he'd thought I was trying to sabotage his mission, and even if he had hated me since we first met as little kids, wouldn't over a decade of the two of us barely tolerating each other have instilled, somewhere deep in his thuggish brain, at least a slight reluctance to slay me?

I tensed when I heard footsteps pounding down the narrow road. I straightened a little to peer over the top of the garbage bin and saw Gordon pitch to a halt in front of the current guard. The guard took his sleeve from his mouth – he'd been trying to bite off a loose thread – and straightened before the breathless Gordon. "You're early," he said in surprise.

"Yeah, I am," Gordon said.

"That's a surprising change," said the guard. "I expected you to be late like usual, sauntering up without even a hint of guilt for making me work an extra ten minutes. How'd you manage to get here before twelve today?"

"Well, you know, you get places faster when you run," said Gordon uncomfortably. His eyes darted over the other guard's shoulders and met mine above the trash bin lid. He gave a slight nod. *Stay put.*

I ducked back down just as the other guard glanced over his shoulder.

"Well, have a good shift," the guard told Gordon. "Everything's been quiet so far today. I almost wish the Dominan assassin would charge to the back door with a sword held high, just to give me something to do. Wouldn't that make this job more exciting?"

I looked around the bin again in time to see Gordon shrug. "I don't know. I sort of like the quiet."

"If you say so," said the guard. "See you, Gordon." And he came marching down the road toward us. I ducked back down and shrank close against the wall, meeting Breesten's eye and putting a warning finger to my lips. For once, Breesten did what I wanted. He pulled his thick limbs as far in as he could and pressed his lips together, holding his breath.

The guard swaggered past. *Don't look back. Don't look back,* I prayed.

The guard stopped. He pulled out his sword.

I held my breath.

He breathed on the blade, shook out his sleeve, and sliced the loose thread neatly with the wicked cutting edge. Then he put his sword away, hurried the rest of the way down the road, and turned the corner without looking back.

I let out my breath.

"Linna!" Gordon called.

I pushed myself to my feet and jogged down to meet him, Breesten at my side.

Gordon paled a bit when he saw that Breesten was with me, but he bravely ignored the fact that Breesten had nearly killed him yesterday and directed his words at me. "Listen, Linna, I can't let you in," he said.

I stiffened. "You said you would."

"I know what I said." He put his hands on his head and pulled at his hair, face twisted with angst. "But it's too dangerous. They – the authorities – know a Dominan's in the city-state. They're going to catch you, and if you're caught and they find out that I agreed to help you, I'll probably be put to death for treason."

"I'll kill you for sure if you don't let us in," Breesten threatened, cocking his fists.

"Let me handle this," I snapped at him. "Gordon, you don't have to worry. With any luck, we'll be gone by the time anyone realizes we were even here."

He shook his head emphatically. "You don't understand – they know who you are. There are pictures of you posted everywhere, Linna, saying that you're part of a Dominan assassination plot and bluffed your way past the guards at the front gates this morning. They're blurry pictures from a security camera above the gates, but you're still easily recognizable. Troops of guards are combing the city-state as we speak, finding people who think they might have seen you and tracking your trail. They'll find you soon."

Breesten whirled on me, uglier than ever with anger. "They're going to find us!" he raged. "They're going to find us, and it's all your fault! You should've been more careful! My mission, ruined... You'll pay for this, Nichols."

He swung a fist, and I would've been knocked flat if my hands hadn't flown up and grabbed his wrist. Growling, he let his left fist fly, but my right elbow whipped out in a blur and blocked the punch.

Despite the adrenaline rushing through my blood, I felt a twinge of pride. Breesten was Fighter number one and I was only number fifty-one, but I could still hold my own in a fistfight.

"You two, stop it! Listen!" cried Gordon.

We froze, and the sound of footsteps coming our way filled my ears. They were crisp, important footsteps, and they sounded like they would turn the corner onto this thin back street in only a few seconds.

I dove back behind the garbage bin, Breesten at my tail.

I spied through the slender crack between the bin and the wall as four guards rounded the corner, and Gordon stepped forward to meet them.

Breesten smacked his gum anxiously, shoving me against the wall as he also tried to see through the crack. "Shh!" I hissed. "They'll hear you!"

He spat his gum into his hand and rolled it like putty between his fingers. I grimaced and pointedly diverted my eyes back through the crack.

"You're awfully young to be a guard, aren't you?" said one of the new guards to Gordon. He, like his companions, held his sword unsheathed and ready in his hand.

Gordon straightened indignantly. "I'm a capable adult, and I've done my job well so far. My mom says I'm probably a more attentive guard than most of King Gerald's other sentries."

"Your mom says?" mocked the new guard. "Well, I think now's the time for you to go back home to your mommy. A Dominan Fighter's loose in Zakarra, and we have reason to believe that the king's life is in great danger. One of us more experienced guards will take your post."

Gordon cast a terrified glance at the trash bin behind which Breesten and I crouched. "You – you don't have to do that," he stammered. "I'm fine. I can handle it." He pulled out his sword and clutched it tightly, as if trying to show his courage.

"Go home, kid," said another of the new guards.

Gordon shook his head. Even from my cramped vantage point behind the trash bin, I saw a bead of sweat slide from under his hair and roll down his face.

"Fine then," said the guard. "You can stand guard here beside me, if it means so much to you. But when a Dominan Fighter charges around the corner with his sword drawn, you'd better stand aside and let *me* handle the fight." He snorted and nodded a goodbye at his companions, who trooped off back around the corner.

I turned to Breesten, who had thankfully dropped his gum and mashed it into the dust. "What do we do now?" I mouthed.

He ignored me, drawing his sword. It sang as it slid from the sheath beneath his jacket, and Gordon and the guard, alerted by the sound, turned in time to see Breesten springing out from behind the garbage bin.

Cold with the fear of Breesten's intents, I lunged after him.

The new guard lifted his sword and countered Breesten's first swipe. The two blades grated against each other like two murderous monsters ramming heads. Breesten's foot thrashed out and cracked nauseatingly against the guard's shin. All color drained from the guard's face as his leg crumpled beneath him. He fell to his knees, sword clattering over the ground, and Breesten stabbed down –

I turned away, but I still heard the awful, squelching crunch as the blade entered the body. I still heard the guard's bubbling last breath rasp away to silence.

Then Gordon made a high-pitched yelping sound. I turned back to him and Breesten, trying to ignore the other guard's crumpled, bleeding body, in time to see Breesten back Gordon against the wall.

"No, no, please," Gordon whimpered as Breesten's sword neared his neck. "I'll help you, I promise. I'm on your side."

"Tack! No!" I yelled.

"I hesitated last time," said Breesten. "But this time..." And he drew his blade across Gordon's throat.

I squeezed my eyes shut, feeling hot bile rise in my throat. I turned to the wall and slumped against it, letting the tiles of the colorful mosaic cut into my arms, and was sick against its base.

Something hit me hard on the back. I spun around to see Breesten's fist retreating, the bloody sword clasped tightly in his other hand. "It's all your fault!" he yelled. "The Zakarrans know we're in the city, and it's all your fault!"

"You killed them!" I yelled back.

"What else was I supposed to do? You weren't any help, standing there like you knew no ways to kill!"

"You *killed* them!"

"So what? I'm a Fighter – it's my job, and it's your job, too! Your father has killed hundreds of enemies! You'd better get used to it!"

"But it's not right!" I tried to explain, shock still coursing through me and making me shake so hard that I had to support myself against the wall. "They were alive, and you just… you killed them!"

"Wake up, Linna!" Breesten bellowed. His sword flashed out, and the flat part of the blade hit my thigh. "This is not a perfect world! You need to get out of whatever imaginary land you've been living in – the land where people don't need to kill in order to survive – and realize that everything worth having is bought with blood!"

I looked down at the bloodstain seeping through my pants. It wasn't my blood. It was Gordon's blood and the blood of the other guard. Even though I tried not to look at the two bodies lying only feet away, the knowledge that they were there made me queasy.

What if Breesten was right? What if killing was a necessary part of life, and I was naïve to think otherwise?

I brushed Breesten out of my way and walked several meters along the wall, putting space between the dead guards and me. I took several deep breaths and tried to erase the image of their bloody corpses from my mind. Then I turned and walked back to Breesten, purposefully keeping my eyes averted from the macabre sight.

"Let's get into the palace," I said. "We're losing time."

He nodded his approval. "Finally, you're seeing sense."

I watched him lift a key from Gordon's lifeless body and open the grilled iron door in the wall, bloodstained sword dangling from his hand. I wondered if he felt any regret for what he'd done, if he felt even a fraction of the shock that still shuddered through me in waves. Maybe he was just good at hiding his emotions, but I thought it more likely that he was still savoring the memory of sword sinking through flesh.

Breesten slipped through the door, and I followed quickly. He locked it behind us and fastened the key on his belt.

I took in the courtyard we had just entered. Exotic trees, red with autumn, hung gracefully over layers of cheery blossoms and vivid leaves. A fountain studded with jewels spat water into a pool darting with brightly colored fish. A smooth, white stone path led to the back door of the palace. I would have found this place peaceful had I not been here on an assassination mission to save my own life.

With a trembling hand, I pulled out my texter and sent Erin a message. *We're in.* I didn't mention Gordon or the other guard, or the revolting way Breesten's sword glistened red. I didn't mention how the bloodstain slapped on my leg by Breesten's blade burned like something evil and still alive.

Breesten stuck his weapon back in its hilt and ran for the back door. He tested the knob. "It's unlocked!" he whooped.

"Keep your voice down," I warned. "There might be people on the other side."

"Oh. Right," he whispered, subdued.

I pressed my ear to the door and quietly shoved it open. A gleaming, modern kitchen met my eyes, and delicious smells wafted through the opening and met my nose. My mouth watered; the waffles I'd eaten for breakfast seemed like a lifetime ago.

"It's a kitchen," I informed Breesten, then closed the door quickly as a man in an apron emerged from behind a pot of popping corn.

"Maybe we should snitch some food," Breesten said.

My stomach grumbled so plaintively that I almost agreed, but then the urgency of our task slammed into me with renewed force. "No," I said. "By the sound of it, there are lots of cooks in there; we need to figure out how to get through the kitchen without being seen."

Breesten's hand flew to his sword. "I can take them," he said.

I blocked the door handle. "No! The less evidence we leave, the better. Don't you think people will become suspicious if there are bloody limbs in their lunches?"

"Oh," he said, obviously disappointed. "I guess you're right."

I cautiously twisted the handle again and peered through the sliver of space between the door and its frame. Food sizzled and popped from within, doubtlessly King Gerald's lunch. Men and women in crisp white aprons bustled to and fro, carrying steaming pans and trays, scrubbing counters, or chopping vegetables with knives that flashed in blurs.

"If we don't kill them, how will we get in?" Breesten asked. "They're everywhere. Someone is sure to see us, and then this mission will be ruined."

I ignored his sulky expression and tried to think. Breesten was probably right, but I would rather sacrifice all my possessions as test subjects for Erin's bombs than admit it. Besides, the thought of more bloodshed made me cringe.

"Let me text Erin," I said.

"Erin!" Breesten spat. "She thinks she's so smart, but she doesn't know anything."

"She's a great Strategist," I retorted loyally.

"She couldn't think of a decent strategy if it broke into her brain," said Breesten. "Once she tried to tell me this plan she had to convince her mom to bake a cake. It involved lighting a garbage can on fire on the curb at the end of my street. It smelled like the end of the world."

I ignored him and briefly texted Erin the situation.

Observe the lowest ranking cooks, she advised. *Also the dishwashers. See if any of them spit in the soup.*

As absurd as this suggestion sounded, I dropped the texter back into my pocket and spied through the cracked opening. Cooks dressed in white crowded past, calling to one another, chopping vegetables, buttering popcorn, and arranging seasoned poultry on shiny white plates.

"What are you doing?" Breesten asked.

"Seeing if anyone spits in the soup," I said. My vision honed in on a bubbling silver pot. Blue flames flashed beneath it, and steam swirled upward from its contents. As I watched, a girl with short hair and a crooked apron gave it a quick stir with a ladle, glanced both ways, and bent over the soup. I couldn't be sure if she spat, but it certainly looked like she might have.

"Don't be thick, Linna," Breesten snapped impatiently. "Nobody's going to spit in the king's soup."

"Someone just did," I said, extracting the texter and typing a new message. I felt smug and victorious, even though I hadn't done anything but follow Erin's instructions.

Find a way to talk to her and ask for her help, Erin wrote.

I pressed my eye to the crack and tracked the girl as she walked away from the soup, straightened her apron, and brushed a blonde curl from her forehead. Her steps were long and purposeful as she gathered a stack of bowls and began filling them with reddish liquid.

"How does this help anything? It'd be faster to fight our way in," Breesten complained. He tried to elbow me out of the way, but I braced myself against the doorframe and continued to observe.

"We need to get into the kitchen and enlist that girl's help," I said, pointing her out to him. "I think – I think maybe I can sneak in and pull her out before the other cooks notice."

"You're insane! You'll give us away!" Breesten snapped. "If that guard I disposed of – Gordon – is to be believed, there are pictures of you hanging on every lamppost in the city-state. Someone will see you and recognize you."

"Fine," I said. "*You* go in then."

"Me?" Breesten squeaked. He coughed and his voice returned to its normal low tone. "Why should I go along with your dimwitted plans? All they've done so far is get us in trouble."

"Just go," I said, too frustrated to argue. "You can even prop the door open a crack so that if anything happens, I can come in and save you." I stepped away from the door and shoved him forward.

"I won't need any help, especially from *you*," Breesten retorted. Scowling, he expanded the door's opening until it was wide enough for his gorilla-like shoulders to squeeze through. No cooks glanced in our direction, at least for the moment. They were absorbed in seasoning King Gerald's popcorn to perfection. Even though he had insisted that he wouldn't need my assistance, I noticed Breesten followed my direction and left the door slightly ajar.

"Hey! You!" The words in the kitchen flew so sharply that even from my safe post outside the door, my heart jumped into my mouth. Breesten spun around and found himself face to face with a short, plump, red-faced cook bearing a wooden spoon like a scepter.

"Where's your apron, ruffian?" the cook demanded, his tall white hat quivering. "And look at those hands! Filthy!"

Breesten stuck his hands in his pockets before the cook could see that the filth on them was blood.

"Well, ruffian? Are you going to wash your hands and find an apron *this instant,* or are you going to lose your job?"

In any other circumstance, I would have laughed out loud to see Breesten looking so uncomfortable.

"Answer me, ruffian!"

"I'll wash my hands and get an apron," Breesten mumbled. Then, when the cook raised his spoon, he hastily added a shouted "Sir!"

The cook lowered his spoon and grunted in grudging satisfaction. "Good," he said. "But if I ever see you in such a state in my kitchen again, I'll kick you out the door so hard you'll fly over the city-state's walls. Is that understood, ruffian?"

"Um, yeah. Understood, sir."

I struggled to keep from laughing aloud as I watched Breesten rinse his hands under a stream of hot water from the sink and awkwardly tie an apron about his torso. The plethora of embarrassments to which he had subjected me the last several years were worth his tortured expression as he began to chop carrots under the watchful eye of the spoon-wielding cook. His prowess with a sword had not helped his vegetable cutting skills in the least.

As the cook lost interest in him and strode off to terrorize another defenseless kitchen hand, Breesten scooted several meters down the counter at which he was working so that he stood across from the girl who was stirring the soup. Their two faces were separated by a veil of steam. My heart thumped wildly as I hoped that Breesten would follow Erin's plan exactly – otherwise, our mission could fail with him in a flowered apron and me lurking outside the door.

Breesten's lips moved, but he spoke so softly that I couldn't hear his words through the cacophony of kitchen noises and the wooden door. The girl's head lifted a little, so I assumed she made some reply.

Breesten glanced over his shoulder to make sure the stout cook was not looking his direction, looked back at the girl, and motioned toward the door with his head. The two crept from the posts, and a few seconds later they joined me in the courtyard.

"Quick," I said, as the wide-eyed girl reeled, bewildered, from Breesten to me. "Let's hide behind that fountain so no one will see us if they look out."

The girl waited till we were hidden, crouched on the white stone path behind the jewel-studded fountain, before speaking. "Who are you?" she asked me. "I've seen your face before, somewhere, but I can't think of where. And *you* – " Now she spoke to Breesten – "surely there's a better way to get a kitchen servant to step outside than to threaten her with death!"

"Tack!" I said, appalled.

"Who are you?" the girl asked again. Now that I could see her face, I found that she was only about my age, maybe a year or two older and an inch or two taller, and the clothes beneath her apron were worn and too big for her.

"My name's Linna," I said. "This is Tack." I tried to keep my voice light as I said, "We're Dominan Fighters and are here to kill the king."

The girl's eyes widened and her lips parted, and for a horrible instant I was afraid she was going to scream. But all she said was, "Why are you telling me this?"

It suddenly felt enormously foolish to confide in this girl; just because she'd spit in the king's soup, it didn't mean that she was prepared to help murder him. There was nothing we could do if she blabbed except kill her, and somehow I couldn't imagine plunging a sword into her heart as being a very clandestine method of quieting a witness. Besides, the deaths of Gordon and his fellow guard still burned in my mind, and I was not eager to see more blood anytime within the next ten million years.

"We need help," I said, deciding that if we'd followed Erin's plan this far, we might as well plunge in all the way. "We know that you hate the king."

"No," she whispered, but her dismayed expression rendered her words useless. She looked like she'd just been caught in a crime. It was obvious that her allegiance to King Gerald was out of fear and duty rather than devotion.

"Don't worry," I said, sensing her alarm that we knew of her disloyalty. "If you cooperate, we won't let anyone know that you even spoke to us. No one will need to know your role in the king's assassination."

The word *assassination* seemed to change something insider her. "I do hate King Gerald," she said. "But I haven't always hated him. Two years ago, my mom lost her job because he decided public schools didn't need so many teachers. I had to find a job as a servant in his kitchen to help feed my younger siblings. It's torture, working in the palace. King Gerald's been sick the whole time I've worked here, so he orders the most extravagant dishes and doesn't even show his face to eat or express his appreciation. I'd quit this job and starve if my brothers and sisters didn't need to eat too."

I felt sorry for her. King Gerald sounded awful, but was he nefarious enough that she actually wanted him dead? She must have read the doubt on my face.

"That's not the worst of it," she said. "My dad used to work in the palace kitchen too. But one day – about eight months ago – as he carried a goblet of wine to the table, he tripped over a dropped fork and spilled wine all over the Head Advisor Piardak's lap." She swallowed, eyebrows drawing together. "Apparently, the suit had been King Gerald's birthday present to Piardak, and the king was furious that it was ruined. The next day, he ordered my father executed."

I stared at her in horror.

"Hundreds of others have been executed in the last two years for offenses just as petty," she said. "I hate

King Gerald. I *hate* him. I want him dead, and if he had an heir, I would want him dead too."

Obviously impatient, Breesten interrupted her by banging his fist against the side of the fountain. "Enough talk," he said. "Can you get us in?"

"I don't know," the girl said falteringly.

"If not, I'll have to finish you off." Breesten reached under his jacket for his sword.

"Wait!" the girl and I cried at the same time.

"You can put on my apron," she said, looking at me. "The two of you can dress like kitchen servants and hopefully pass through the kitchen unnoticed. The door from the kitchen leads into the dining room. Piardak and some aristocrats will be dining there; you can carry out some dishes, lay them on the table, and exit through the door that leads into the hall. Hopefully, none of the diners will notice that you don't return to the kitchen."

I bit my lip and looked at Breesten. I knew this was a risky plan, and Erin could probably think of something better, but I didn't want to hide behind the fountain and deliberate – I wanted to kill the king and get out of Zakarra as soon as I could.

"Okay," I agreed, knowing I had no choice but to trust this girl. "Let's get it over with."

The girl gave me her apron, and I slipped it over my head and tied it clumsily at the back. It seemed like a poor disguise, and I hoped fervently that nobody I'd encounter in the palace's kitchen or dining room would have been outside recently enough to have seen the posters with my face.

"Just pretend that you know what you're doing," said the girl. "The bowls of soup should be on the far counter, ready to deliver to the table. Make sure to serve Piardak first."

I nodded, hands clammy, and approached the door that led to the kitchen, each step feeling like one stride closer to my doom.

Breesten slipped through the door first, and I stayed right at his tail. Nobody offered so much as a sideways glance in our direction as we did our best to wear our aprons like badges of belonging.

We maneuvered through the bustling cooks and finally found the back counter. Sure enough, ten bowls of the soup the girl had spat in sat ready to serve on its marble surface. I found two trays and loaded five bowls on each.

"What do you think you're doing, ruffian?" barked an authoritative voice from behind me. I nearly dropped the tray, but my fingers just managed to catch the edges before it slipped from my grasp. A couple droplets splattered over the sides of the bowls and dripped onto the delicately embossed serving dish.

"Taking the diners their soup," I said. My voice sounded strangled; the red-faced, spoon-bearing cook had backed me against the counter.

"You fool!" he bellowed. "You've forgotten the spoons!"

"The spoons?" I echoed dumbly, relieved that he hadn't realized I was an imposter.

"Yes!" he raged. "The spoons! You can't expect the royal diners to enjoy their soup without the proper silverware!"

I opened my mouth – I didn't know what I was going to say, probably something about how I'd get the spoons right away – but I never got the chance to speak. Breesten pulled out his sword and, with a grunt, swung it at the cook's head.

The cook ducked, narrowly avoiding decapitation. Breesten's sword sliced his tall white hat and sent it flying into the stove, where it promptly caught fire, turned black, and curled to ashes.

"Kitchen workers! This ruffian is trying to ruin the royal lunch! Catch him!" the cook yelled.

Kitchen servants shrieked, and a few dishwashers dropped the forks they were polishing. They scrambled chaotically over the floor in an attempt to pick them back up, and someone lobbed an apple at Breesten's face, which he cleaved neatly in two with his sword. A scowling cook manning a nearby stir-fry lifted his steaming, sizzling frying pan and held it threateningly, posed to hurl it at Breesten.

"Stop!" I yelled, grabbing a knife from a nearby vegetable-chopper's hand. I darted in front of Breesten and pointed the knife at the cook with the pan. "If you even look like you're about to throw that at us, I'll throw this into your heart," I said.

"Don't listen to her! She's with that other ruffian – they want to sabotage the lunch!" The cook Breesten had almost killed swung his spoon wildly about. Without his hat, I could see the large bald spot on top of his round head.

"I don't!" I insisted as the man with the pan stepped closer, forcing a young dishwasher to duck so as not to hit his head against the scalding metal. "I don't want to sabotage the lunch! Put that thing down before you hurt someone!"

But, of course, he didn't listen; instead he advanced, frying pan held before him, until the searing surface hung less than two inches from my face. Even if I'd been able to collect enough courage to kill him, my hands were so sweaty that I couldn't find a proper grip on the knife.

The cook brought the pan still closer; now I could feel its heat on my face, reddening my skin. "Why are you trying to ruin the king's lunch?" he demanded, his voice cold and unforgiving.

"I'm not," I whimpered. For once, Breesten remained silent. I wished he would speak up; fear had bunted all logic from my brain and I couldn't think up a good excuse. I decided to tell the truth. The mission was over now, anyway. We had been discovered.

"We don't want to ruin his lunch," I said. "We want to kill him."

His expression changed. His lips parted in surprise, his eyebrows lifted out of his scowl, and the livid purple hue drained from his cheeks. "You mean…" his voice trailed off for a second before he found it again. "You mean that you're the Dominan Fighters? Both of you?"

I nodded and wondered if he was still going to brand my face with the frying pan. His grip on it had relaxed, and to my intense relief, he lowered it back onto the stove. "It's all right!" he called out to the rest of the cooks and kitchen servants. "They're not trying to ruin the royal lunch – they want to kill the king!"

The kitchen erupted into cheers. Breesten and I exchanged an astonished look. Did so many people really despise King Gerald?

The now hatless cook with the spoon embraced Breesten and me in a spice-scented hug. "Let me guess," he said. "You need to get through the dining room to get to the palace's hall beyond."

"Yeah," I stammered. "We planned to go to the dining room as though we were employed servants, serve the king's second-in-command and his guests their soup, and exit through the door that leads to the hall."

"A good plan," said the cook. "Just make sure you serve Piardak first."

"How will we know which one is Piardak?" I asked.

"You'll know. He'll be the one at the end of the table in some sort of hideously expensive suit. He has a mouth like an alligator."

I picked up a tray of soup in one hand, but when I tried to set my knife on the counter, the cook stopped me. "Is something dead in your head, ruffian?" he asked. "Don't put that down! Not everyone in the palace is as kindly toward assassins as us cooks; you might need a weapon."

So I stuck the knife in my belt, Breesten hid his sword back under his jacket, and, each holding a tray of soup, we stepped into the royal dining room.

All conversation ceased as we entered with the appetizer. At least a dozen royal diners lounged around the largest table I had ever seen. It was rectangular, but the corners were slightly rounded and it was made completely of glass. The top was transparent, giving the eerie impression that the plates and folded napkins hung in midair, and the table legs were various shades of glistening red, blue, and green. A chandelier hung from the ceiling, an astounding artifact of top-notch electrical engineering. Shards of light danced on the faces of the diners, giving the room a mystical appearance.

"Finally!" boomed the man at the head of the table. "The soup is ready!" He wore a swishy silver suit made of soft silk, and his teeth were very sharp and white. I agreed with the cook's description; he looked like an alligator.

Trying not to reveal the trembling in my hands, I took a bowl of soup from the tray and set it before Piardak along with a spoon. I didn't know if the king's second-in-command was accustomed to people bowing – people rarely, if ever, bowed to the Governor in Domina – so I dipped my head respectfully in a compromise and hurried around the table to distribute the other four bowls of soup. Breesten maladroitly served the bowls on his tray, and though I winced at his clumsiness, he miraculously didn't spill a drop.

Piardak didn't say anything. He simply dipped into his soup, and his ten or twelve guests followed his example.

I elbowed Breesten and nodded toward the door – not the small, nondescript door to the kitchen, but the grand, heavily engraved wooden door which I knew would lead into the royal hall.

Slowly, quietly, purposefully, we walked toward that door. My legs felt wobbly, like the muscles had been replaced by gelatin. Hopefully, Piardak and the other diners were too absorbed in the spicy pepper-saliva soup to give us any attention.

I opened the door. It swung to accommodate us without a sound. We slipped through and stood blinking in an empty hall with lush, intricately patterned carpets and a sweeping staircase at one end. "Let's hurry," I whispered, moving for the staircase, but Breesten stopped me.

"No," he hissed. "We take the back stairs. That's what Tomkins told me."

"Why?" I asked. "Do you even know where the back stairs are?" My disdain toward Tomkins was stronger than ever, having been fueled by Erin's many infallible strategies over the past thirty-six hours.

Breesten scratched at his stiff clumps of hair and said, "The front entrance is to our right, so the back entrance should be to our left. Around the corner, past the discussion room, and at the end of the hall."

Despite my grudge against him and his overly exalted Strategist, I couldn't help but be impressed. I tried to cover my admiration by muttering, "Then hurry up and get to the next floor."

Mumbling foul remarks about me under his breath, Breesten obliged. We turned left, tiptoed to the far end of the hall, and rounded the corner to find ourselves in a narrower corridor, the left-hand wall interrupted at regular intervals by closets and closed doors. At the end I saw a dim, steep staircase.

I knew it wouldn't take long to reach the stairs, but I was sick with fear that one of the doors along the hall would open and someone would step out to discover us before we got to them. We'd have to be fast. Without glancing at Breesten, I burst into a sprint.

His feet pounded after me, and within a few seconds he pulled ahead. The days in which I could outrun him in the fifty-meter dash had ended long ago. He reached the staircase, bounded halfway up the charcoal-gray steps, and panted over his shoulder, "Faster, Linna!"

Fear and adrenaline choked me, turning my mouth cold and metallic. I caught up to him and we scurried up the remaining steps. I was worried they would creak, but King Gerald's palace was in good condition. The sturdy wooden stairs remained robust and made no protest.

We paused for a moment on the top landing. Breesten obstinately ignored me. I wished for the millionth time that Erin stood at my side instead of him. With Erin, I would feel safe and confident. She would know what to do next, and I wouldn't have to worry that she would run off and leave me to fend for myself. But the only companion I had was Breesten, and he probably wished that he'd run me through with his sword when he'd had the chance.

"What now?" I asked.

He spoke to me through gritted teeth, like he was trying to explain something obvious to an annoying child. "We've reached the second floor. Now we need to get to the third floor. And then the fourth floor. Then finally the fifth floor so we can sneak into King Gerald's bedchamber and I can stab him."

I glanced around for another staircase, but there was none in sight. "How do we accomplish that?"

"The stairs to the next floor are on the other side of the palace," he said. "They alternate, so we'll have to cross every floor to get to the next flight."

Tomkins must have found that out and told him. Even stronger than my anger at the fact that he knew more about the layout of the palace than I did was my antipathy at the self-important way he uttered his knowledge.

I tried not to reveal the fact that I wished Breesten and Tomkins would both be eaten alive by rabid saber-toothed monkeys and nodded. As we began to trek down the long, thickly carpeted hall, I dug out the texter and sent Erin a new message. *We're on the second floor. Any advice?*

Her reply appeared so quickly that it was a wonder she'd managed to type it all. *I have Tomkins's mission file in front of me. There's a map of the palace. Just walk straight through – I don't think you'll have any trouble as long as you clearly announce your business.*

I wanted to type back not to be ridiculous. We were on a covert mission; we didn't want to parade through the palace informing everyone that we were going to kill their king. Maybe Erin was a genius, but sometimes her suggestions seemed extraordinarily impractical.

Before I could tap this into the texter's tiny screen, one of the doors on the left-hand side of the hallway opened. I bumped into Breesten, who had frozen, and tried to turn myself invisible. Unfortunately, invisibility was not an advantage that Dominan Fighters possessed.

An old, wrinkled man peered at us from the doorway. He scrunched up his forehead in confusion, adding even more creases to his face. "What are you two doing out of the kitchen?" he asked.

I glanced down and realized that the apron was still tied around my waist. Breesten's hand crept under his jacket, but I elbowed him sharply in the ribs, and he quit trying to pull out his sword.

"Are you trying to dodge your duties as royal kitchen hands?" roared the old man. His raisin-like hands clenched into fists at his sides. "Do you dare to insult the king by disregarding your assigned tasks?"

His voice had aroused the interest of other servants. Doors on the left and right creaked open, and dozens of curious servants poked their heads from their rooms to see what had caused the commotion.

Some of them carried knives or clubs. One of them held a plastic dustpan above his head, ready to strike.

I turned to Breesten. My mouth had gone dry.

"Run," he whispered.

But when we turned to race to the end of the corridor, we found our path obstructed by an army of servants. Every one of them glared at us with complete loathing. We were trapped.

~ 9 ~

"We're dead," I mumbled. I didn't know if Breesten heard, but his hand crept under his jacket. I knew he was clenching the handle of his sword.

"Did Erin make any suggestions?" he asked tersely. His tone made it obvious that he doubted Erin could rescue us from this situation.

I remembered Erin's advice to plainly state that we were here to kill the king. It was a careless plan. My throat tightened as I stared at the wall of servants. They looked ready to fight – even to kill – in order to keep us from reaching King Gerald.

"Why are you not in the kitchen?" demanded the wrinkled man again. "Do you find it amusing to be negligent toward the king's meals?"

"No," said Breesten. He pulled out his sword. "But what we're up to is none of your business. So stand out of the way or feel the wrath of my sword!" He swung, and several servants hopped out of the way before the gleaming blade could slice off their heads. But then a rebellious freckle-nosed teenager chucked something that looked like a bowling ball at us. It smashed into the floor, missing Breesten's foot by centimeters.

"Attack these insurgents!" he cried, and soon the air was thick with flying missiles. I dodged a pair of shoes, a toilet plunger, and a handful of marbles before ducking behind Breesten's beefy frame for safety. He held his sword in front of his face, deflecting the objects but unable to attack for fear of being hit in the face by a flying encyclopedia.

"This is ridiculous!" I yelled.

"This is completely your fault!" he replied.

I didn't know how he came to that conclusion, but I was too busy pulling the texter from my pocket to care. With Breesten's bulk acting as a bulwark from the servants' lobbed projectiles, I tapped out a brief message to Erin: *The servants are attacking! What should we do?*

It only took her a few seconds to respond, but in my blast of panic, it seemed like years.

I told you. Tell the truth.

"You're insane!" I yelled at the words on the screen, even though I knew Erin couldn't hear me.

But then two more words appeared. *Trust me.*

I ducked as a feather duster whizzed by my ear, clutching the texter and trying to keep Breesten in front of me as a shield. "We're not kitchen servants!" I cried, yelling to be heard above the mob's roar. "We're here to kill – "

Breesten immediately swung around and plunged his sword at my chest. I barely twisted away in time to keep from getting impaled; that was the second time he'd tried to kill me. Why couldn't I have ended up with a more mild-mannered companion?

I gasped a new breath of oxygen and tried again. "We're here – "

Whoosh! Breesten's sword sailed over my head, brushing my ponytail as I crouched just in time.

"We're here to kill – "

I threw myself flat on the floor as Breesten made a second, lower swipe. The whistling blade rippled my jacket with a breeze.

"We're here to kill the king!"

I rolled frantically as I saw the blur of Breesten's blade descend, and the sword stabbed into the carpet and stuck there right where my body had been a moment before. As Breesten, panting and growling, yanked his weapon out of the floor, I prepared to either be sliced to death by his sword or fatally stoned by servants with random paraphernalia now that they knew I had come to murder their beloved King Gerald.

"Quit trying to kill her, you brainless gorilla!" the wrinkled old man yelled, chucking a bottle of mustard at Breesten. It hit him in the shoulder, burst open, and splattered down the front of his apron. Miraculously, he obeyed, breathing heavily and trying to slip the flowered apron off over his head.

The servants had lowered their objects and now stood scrutinizing us. "You're the Dominan Fighters?" one of them asked in disbelief.

I nodded, and Breesten glowered.

I thought they were going to raise their missiles again and murder us, but instead they began to cheer. "Hallelujah!" shouted the wrinkled man. The way he cheered was beautiful, like he had been waiting all his life to utter this word. And even though I had no idea what this word meant, a tingle ran down my spine as it rolled off his tongue in splendid syllables like something more lovely than music.

He rushed forward and shook my hand ecstatically. "I've been working in this palace for thirty years," he informed us, "and never have I been able to oppose the king. But now with your help..." His eyes filled with tears of joy and his voice ceased to work.

I grabbed the sword from Breesten's hand and held it at my side. If he decided he wanted to kill me after all, I didn't want to have to duck his swinging blade. "You're not going to stop us?" I asked. "You're not loyal to King Gerald?"

He laughed scornfully. "Loyal to the king? I've never been loyal to him. Well, if you'd asked me a few years ago I might've said I was, but that was before the guy stopped even trying to *seem* like he was helping his people."

"He deserves to be killed!" a thin young man called out. "And if you're the assassins, you are our saviors!"

"I'm going to kill him," Breesten said, snatching his sword back from me like he was afraid I'd steal his glory. "*I'm* going to."

The wrinkled old man dipped his head in respect, and all the other servants followed his example. Breesten swelled with pride, eyes gleaming as brightly as his sword, looking like he was in the middle of a dream from which he never wanted to wake.

Then a quaver-eyed woman behind the wrinkled man tentatively lifted her voice. "We all hate King Gerald," she said, "but... do we really want to *kill* him?"

"What d'you mean?" Breesten barked. "If you're faithful to the king, it'd be wise to shut your mouth now before I shut it with my sword."

Before I knew what I was doing, I elbowed Breesten hard and said, "Let her talk, Tack." I didn't know why, but suddenly my heartbeat had quickened. I needed to hear what this woman had to say.

"I – I'm not saying that King Gerald isn't an evil man," she said, speaking cautiously now that everyone's eyes were on her. "He is evil, but he's still human – he's still a person like you or me. He's *alive*. How can one person snuff out another's life? What gives one person the right to kill another man who has laughed and cried just like everyone else, who was once a chubby baby like my little nephew or a gangly young man like my son Gordon?"

I felt like something poisonous had smacked my insides as I realized the woman was Gordon's mother. The dried bloodstain on my pants started to burn against my leg, and my hand crept down to cover it, to hide the screaming proof of the poor guard's death from the woman who had loved him more than anyone else.

"Are you saying that we should continue to let King Gerald oppress us?" challenged the man with the wrinkled face. He scowled, and dark crevasses lined his features. "He's been making our lives miserable for years, and you don't want to stop him?"

Gordon's mother wrung her hands. "I'm not saying that I like him," she defended herself. "I just don't think it's right to kill him."

I wondered what she would say if she knew that, earlier today, Breesten had murdered her son.

Breesten stepped forward. I noticed that the muscles were tensed in his sword arm. "Are you loyal to King Gerald?" he demanded. "If you oppose me – a Dominan Fighter – you will pay with your life!"

Specks of dried blood still stained the metal blade at his side. Gordon's blood. The lady glanced down at the sword; her face betrayed no knowledge that this weapon had stolen the life from her son. Suddenly, I decided I needed to leave this mob of servants as quickly as possible.

"Come on, Tack," I said, grabbing the sleeve of his jacket and tugging him toward the end of the hallway. 'Let's go. We don't have much time."

He slapped my hand away and turned back to the curious cluster of servants. "Do not mention this to anyone," he warned. "There will be dire consequences if any of you pitiful peasants ruin our...*my* mission." With a threatening flourish of his sword, he hurried after me.

"That was Gordon's mother!" I hissed as we bounded up the next staircase.

"Who?" he asked dumbly.

"Gordon's mother!" I repeated. "Remember Gordon? The guard you slaughtered?"

Breesten stomped indignantly. "I didn't *slaughter* him. I disposed of him nobly because he stood in our way. Any other *worthy* Fighter would have done the same."

The way he emphasized the word *worthy* made it plain that he was not referring to me. I didn't care; the sooner this mission was completed and we could go home, the better.

I wondered how my father would react if I died in the attempt to assassinate the Zakarran king. He would probably be outraged that I had disobeyed him by sneaking into Zakarra. Perhaps he would be too livid to mourn my demise. I reminded myself that if the king was not successfully murdered before midnight tonight, he was going to have me executed anyway.

Our voices fell as we approached the top of the stairs; I had no idea what awaited us on the third floor, but I doubted it would be as welcoming as the servants had been. I pulled my apron over my head and left it in a crumpled ball on a step. This far from the palace kitchen, that disguise would be useless.

"Hold on," I told Breesten, pulling my texter out again. He rolled his eyes but halted long enough for me to tap out a message to Erin. *Third floor. What should we do?*

Do you like birds? she texted back.

At first I was puzzled, but then I remembered Erin telling me that King Gerald had a pet emu. Perhaps the king had given it the third floor as a space to roam. I looked up at Breesten. "Emus aren't dangerous, are they?" I asked.

His face scrunched up under his coarse clumps of messy hair. "What's an emu? Some sort of weapon?"

For the thousandth time, I wondered how someone so obtuse had been made Fighter number one. I thought of the small, flitting birds and the majestic eagles I'd seen in Domina. None of them seemed particularly vicious, unless you were a rodent who happened to look like an eagle's tasty snack. I felt the kitchen knife in my belt. The thought of killing a human revolted me; would slaughtering an animal be any easier? As long as the emu left us alone, Breesten and I should be able to cross the third floor without any trouble.

I darted past Breesten and led the rest of the way up the stairs. At the top I emerged into what looked like an indoor park. Dazzling green leaves, larger than any I'd ever seen, danced against the ceiling where they sprouted from lofty trees, and fine sand lay two inches deep over the floor.

"Is this the king's private indoor zoo or something?" Breesten muttered, twirling his sword to shred a thorny bush that had snagged his pant leg.

I shrugged, wondering why any sane individual would go to so much trouble to import these exotic plants. Suddenly, a booming call split through the indoor forest. It echoed through the capacious chamber, startling and distinctly inhuman, like the kind of sound I'd always imagined a dinosaur or dragon might make.

"What was that?" Breesten asked jumpily.

"I think that's the call of the emu," I said, shivering. What sort of bird could make such a horrible noise?

"Let's hurry," Breesten urged. I noticed that perspiration dampened his horn-like clumps of hair. He began to run and I followed, trying to avoid branches that tried to snag my hair and whack me in the face.

Suddenly Breesten let out a howl of panic. The biggest bird I'd ever seen erupted from the trees, ridiculously tiny wings flapping and long, thin legs clawing the ground. Another booming call blasted from its throat like a deafening projectile.

"Hold still!" I ordered Breesten. We both froze, and my chest rose and fell fearfully as the emu eyed us warily, its beady eyes scrutinizing as it debated whether to attack. I was agonizingly aware of the scalpel-like nails on its talons. The bird stood so close that I could see its every detail – its dark, shaggy feathers, round head, and frowning beak. The emu was taller than I was, and it probably weighed almost as much. A metal collar glinted on its long, sparsely feathered neck.

"I'll kill it," Breesten whispered. He reached for his sword.

At his movement the emu shouted again, flapping its wings in a gigantic flurry of feathers.

Breesten fumbled for his sword, and my hands scrabbled to my belt to pull out my knife, which I held in two hands before me to guard my face should the emu try to attack.

Then Breesten shrieked, "There's another!"

I spun my head, ponytail whipping my neck, and saw he was right – a second monstrous bird, also with a collar around its neck, stepped from behind a tree and joined its companion.

"How many are there?" Breesten whimpered. "I hate birds, especially insanely *big* birds."

"Let's back up really slowly," I suggested, trying to keep my voice calm so as not to incite the emus to charge. I eased my foot backward through the sand and inched my body slowly back a step. Breesten copied my movement, still clutching his sword, and the emus watched us with their beady, unreadable eyes. "Another step," I breathed, and Breesten and I took it in unison. Slowly and anxiously, sliding our shoes backward through the dust on the ground with each step, we began to move away from the staring birds. I didn't like the way their heads moved as they studied us. They might have been conversing in a silent emu language, discussing how tasty two Dominan Fighters would be for lunch.

"I can kill them," Breesten insisted, licking sweat from his upper lip.

"We don't need to," I whispered, straining to keep my voice low and composed. "This is working fine. Just keep backing up."

Even though all my strength was focused on shuffling away from the birds, a small part of my brain felt relief that there were no security guards to challenge us on this level.

"Are they carnivorous?" Breesten asked.

"I don't know," I replied. I tried to recall any knowledge I'd ever absorbed about outlandish, gargantuan birds, but my education seemed strangely lacking in that subject. Why had my teachers never bothered to explain the eating habits of emus?

The emus watched us warily, but they made no move to attack. I ground my teeth in frustration. It seemed ridiculous that we had come this far only to have our mission hindered by two oversized featherbrains. "Let's just walk past them," I suggested, mustering my courage.

"No way," Breesten said. "They'll tear us apart. Look at those talons!"

I intractably tried not to notice the sharp claws on the ends of the birds' feet. "Just act confident," I said, more to myself than to Breesten, and then I began to step forward.

"Linna!" Breesten moaned. He sounded more like a scared kid than a highly ranked Fighter. I would have laughed if I hadn't been so concerned about startling the emus.

"Come on," I urged impatiently. One of the emus stepped forward to block my path. Its gleaming collar was dotted with rhinestones – actually, they were probably real diamonds – that spelled out its name. *Kayla*.

I decided not to wonder how such a fierce-looking animal could have been given such a pleasant moniker. I'd expected something like *Killer* or *Bloodbeak*. "Good Kayla," I purred. "What a nice bird. Just let us pass to the other side, and then we'll leave you alone."

Kayla bobbed her head, interested by the sound of my voice.

"Its name is *Kayla?*" said Breesten in disbelief.

"Yeah," I said. "Tell her what a good emu she is."

Breesten's voice sounded strangled as he choked out, "Good emu, Kayla. Don't hurt us. What... um... lovely talons you have. They're so sharp and deadly. You must be very proud of your talons."

That was just like Breesten, I decided. He could never think of anything to talk about besides lethal weapons.

As Breesten awkwardly crooned to Kayla, I turned my attention to the other emu. Its collar said its name was Abby.

"Nice Abby," I muttered. "Who gave you that name, huh? Did King Gerald name you? Is he going loopy in his old age?"

"Steady, Kayla," Breesten said. "That's it, don't attack us. Good girl. You don't want to attack us. Because if you do, I'll cut you to bits."

Kayla cocked her head, but she gave no indication that she'd comprehended the threat. "Nice words only, Tack," I warned. "I don't know how smart these emus are."

As we walked through the forest, the emus tagged along behind us. Their eyes tracked every move we made. It seemed like they were sizing us up, ready to strike. Or perhaps they were just curious to know what two foreign Fighters were doing in their domain.

As we walked, I typed a new message to Erin. *Walking through the emus' floor. Their names are Kayla and Abby. Is the king insane?*

Erin's response did little to convince me of her own sanity. *Probably. Give them kisses for me. And be careful on the fourth floor.*

I stared at the emus in disgust. There was no way I was going to smooch those beasts. *What's on the fourth floor?*

Ice cream. Don't eat any, she said.

I shoved the texter in my pocket, more than a little annoyed at Erin's evasive answers. Didn't she know that after risking my neck countless times on this mission already, I had no tolerance left for her flippancy?

Finally the stairs came into sight behind a tangle of shrubs. I spoke soothingly to the emus while Breesten hacked the shrubs away with his sword to reveal that a wire fence blocked the passage to the staircase, presumably to keep the emus from wandering to the fourth floor.

"Can you cut it away with your sword?" I asked. Breesten nodded grimly and set to work on the fence.

"Good Kayla. Good Abby," I said. It felt weird to talk to hideous birds in a crooning voice – I'd never babied anything, person or animal, in my life. My dad had certainly never given an example of mollycoddling for me to follow. "You've been very well-behaved emus so far. That gorilla just needs to break an opening through the fence so we can go assassinate your greedy owner, King Gerald. Okay?"

The way the emus watched me with their nodding, serious, beaked faces almost made me think they understood.

"It's clear!" Breesten announced, wrenching a last bit of metal wire aside to reveal a hole big enough to squirm through. He wriggled into the stairwell and I backed through after him, keeping my eyes on the two emus as I did so.

"Emus aren't so bad," I told Breesten as we clambered toward the fourth floor.

"Overgrown poultry," he muttered darkly. "I should've slashed off their heads. I'm not eating chicken again for a long time." Then he looked at me sharply. "I wasn't scared, of course. It'd be crazy to be scared of such silly-looking things."

I nodded, deciding it wouldn't be worth it to argue.

"Does Erin have any advice about the fourth floor?" Breesten asked. I noticed that his tone had lost a little of its disdain for my best friend's strategies.

I tried not to betray my annoyance with Erin as I said, "She told me not to eat any ice cream."

"Well, she's just loads of help," said Breesten sarcastically.

"She might have a good reason for saying that," I said, trying to stand up for my friend. "Maybe the ice cream is poisoned. Maybe eating it will give us stomachaches and then we won't be able to run fast enough to get away from some guard later."

"Why would there be ice cream on the fourth floor when the kitchen and the dining room are both on the first floor?" Breesten pointed out. That silenced me. Maybe Erin really didn't know what she was talking about. Maybe the ice cream message had just been a joke, trying to keep my spirits up.

"Well, let's get through this level quickly and get to the king's chambers," I said, trying to change the subject.

We stepped onto the fourth floor. I breathed a sigh of relief. We were almost there – hopefully we would reach King Gerald's bedchamber within a few minutes.

I raised my eyes to see what awaited us on this level and found myself staring at the biggest ice cream fountain I'd ever seen.

~ 10 ~

I averted my eyes from the ice cream fountain and ignored my sudden craving for frozen dairy products. "No guards," I said, scanning the area. I couldn't believe we had come this far already. I could almost allow myself to believe that the mission would be accomplished. But then I remembered not to get ahead of myself; we still had to enter the king's quarters and assassinate him.

"I'm hungry, Linna," said Breesten, eyeing the fountain.

"No," I said firmly. "You are not going to waste time by getting a snack." I thought of Erin's advice and knew that she was right; stopping to snitch some royal ice cream would only distract us from our task.

"I'm going to eat some," Breesten said stubbornly.

He was only acting so mulish to show his rancor toward Erin. I shook my head. "We're so close, Tack. Let's just get it over with and you can eat when we get back to Domina."

He shoved me away from him. "Don't boss me around, Linna. That's the reason you're so annoying; just because you're the Governor's daughter, you think you can tell everyone else what to do."

He marched to the ice cream fountain and licked his lips as he surveyed the fifty-seven flavors and eighty-three choices of toppings. "Ugh," he muttered. "Linna, there's a *broccoli* flavored ice cream."

I made a face. "Let's go," I said anxiously.

"No, I want some ice cream. Not broccoli ice cream, though." He found the spout for chocolate-chip ice cream, grabbed an enormous bowl from the convenient rack, and pulled the lever.

Instant pandemonium erupted. Alarms began blaring, lights started flashing, and voices could be heard pounding toward where we stood.

"Hide!" I yelled. Breesten and I catapulted over the top of the ice cream fountain and crouched in the narrow space between it and the wall. My legs instantly cramped from the tight, uncomfortable position, but I didn't dare to move. Through the crack between the floor and the base of the fountain, I watched to see what drama would unfold.

I wanted to harangue Breesten for alerting the whole palace of our position, but before my tongue could even form the words, guards burst over the top of the stairs and unsheathed their swords.

"Where are they?" one of them demanded. "Where are the Dominan Fighters?"

"Relax, Rudolph," said another, lazily slicing his sword through the air. "Piardak's just paranoid; there's no way Dominans could get into the palace. It's probably simply one of the servants trying to pinch some ice cream."

"Brainless servants," said Rudolph, sneering. "This fountain's reserved for no one but Piardak and King Gerald." He glared at the frosty machine in disgust. "But I wish it hadn't been booby-trapped. I used to sneak a treat once in awhile."

The other guard nodded, but he didn't seem very interested in what Rudolph had to say. He turned to the rest of the palace sentinels. "Let's go back down to the servants' quarters and interrogate them. If we're threatening enough, maybe someone will confess to the crime," he said.

They clambered back down the staircase, some of them muttering about how it was an ignominy that dignified protectors of King Gerald were reduced to mere ice cream watchers.

I waited a few seconds after their voices had faded away to make sure it was safe before clambering back over the fountain, legs aching from crouching in the tiny space. Breesten climbed out after me and threw his bowl down in disgust. "I'm still hungry!" he complained.

"The sooner you kill the king, the sooner you can get back to Domina and get something to eat," I reminded him, patience fraying. "Come on, this floor looks deserted. I bet we can find the staircase without running into anyone."

The fourth floor certainly appeared empty. The room with the ice cream fountain also contained a churning cotton candy machine and a colossal refrigerator which I didn't dare open. In the center of the glossy hardwood floor was an intricately sculpted metal table with a glass top and chairs to match. We tiptoed by the table, careful not to touch anything in case we triggered another alarm, and passed into the next room. At one end sat a stage screened by embroidered silk curtains, and plush recliners lined the opposite wall.

"What's this, the king's private theater?" Breesten said.

"Yeah, this is probably where the circus performed," I said.

"If I kill the king, maybe your dad would be grateful enough to buy me one of these," Breesten said.

I snorted. "To do that, my dad would have to be capable of gratitude."

Breesten gave me a quizzical look and then apparently remembered that we were supposed to be enemies. He resumed his usual stormy expression. "You're making too much noise. The guards are going to hear us."

I chose not to remind him that *he* was the one who'd set off the alarms. We padded through the room, careful not to disturb any of the cushiony recliners, and then walked around the back of the stage. I shoved a fistful of soft curtains aside and pointed at the doorway that had just been revealed.

Breesten nodded, sweat on his forehead and his eyes gleaming with excitement. I felt the way that he looked: a mixture of nerves and anticipation jiggled expectantly in my stomach.

I rattled the doorknob. "Locked!" I whispered. I should've foreseen a complication like this in our plan.

"Is there another door?" Breesten asked. "Maybe this one doesn't lead to the staircase."

We circled the enormous room, palms pressed to the wall in case there was a secret panel, searching for another doorway. Nothing. The only entrance to the fifth floor was blocked off, and surely the guards would soon realize that none of the servants had tried to steal King Gerald's ice cream. When they found that there were intruders in the palace, they would undoubtedly storm into this room and kill us on the spot.

"Can you force the lock?" Breesten asked.

I braced myself against the wall and twisted the knob, throwing all my weight against the wooden panel. "No," I said. "It's too strong."

"Let me try." Breesten cracked his knuckles, causing me to wince, and waited for me to step out of the way. Then he smashed his muscular frame into the door with a thud, causing the wood to shudder.

"Try again," I urged.

He battered his weight into the door again, but to no avail. "The door's too sturdy," he said. I could see the disappointment in his face. Breesten prided himself on his muscles; it was an insult to his strength to be bested by a piece of carpentry.

I turned to make sure no guards were approaching. We were still undiscovered, but I didn't know how long that would last. "Can we pick the lock?" I asked.

Breesten shrugged. "With what?"

I pulled a bobby pin from my hair and inserted it into the keyhole. Nothing happened as I wriggled it around – the tip didn't fit into the mechanism. "No use," I said, wondering if we would have to accept defeat. "It's too big for the hole."

Breesten pulled out his sword from under his jacket with a flourish. Catching sight of his dogged expression, for a moment I thought he was going to try to murder me again. But he just elbowed me out of the way and slipped the sharp, thin end of the blade into the crack between the door and its frame.

"Good idea," I admitted grudgingly as he began to saw away at the bolt that held the door closed. With a grinding sound and a loud click, the lock fell away and we grinned at each other in relief before remembering that we were supposed to be bitter enemies.

I expected a staircase to greet us on the other side of the door, but when I thrust myself through the opening, a fresh breeze rippled through my hair and sudden sunlight forced my eyes to squint.

"I think this is the wrong – " Breesten started, but he stopped abruptly as he caught sight of the three Zakarran guards leaning over the balcony's railing, les than ten feet away. He started making frantic gestures at me, mouthing, *"Don't make a sound."*

I swallowed, eyes locking on the guards' backs. The one in the middle had beefy shoulders, the one on the left was slouched with a jacket too big for his frame, and the one on the right had bristly, gray-streaked hair. If one of them turned his head, we'd be discovered. I started to step back into the palace, but then I saw the staircase only twenty paces to our right, leading to a higher balcony. To get to the next floor, we'd have to walk right past the guards. I knew it was too much to hope that they wouldn't notice us.

What kind of royal architect would create such an incongruous stairwell?

Breesten's arm crept under his jacket, but I delivered a quick kick to his shins. His offended yelp might have given us away if I hadn't flown a finger to my lips. We had been successful in talking our way out of trouble so far. Perhaps if the guards saw us, they'd send us up to carry out the assassination with their blessing. But I didn't want to take that chance.

I reached into my pocket for the texter. Breesten scowled as I tapped out a message to Erin, but he didn't interfere. As I waited for Erin's reply, I watched the guard on the left light a cigarette, bring it to his mouth, and huff, sending gross gray smoke snaking skyward. Breesten and I stared, appalled. We'd never seen anyone smoke before – the habit was prohibited in Domina – and we hadn't realized how repulsive it was.

I looked down to see Erin's reply. *Sit back and wait for the fireworks!*

For a moment I thought she was being metaphorical – until about five seconds later, when the first explosions ripped across the sky.

The guards jumped so suddenly that my insides shook with suppressed laughter. "Bombs!" one yelled. They leaned over the railing, staring at the sky. The smoker dropped his cigarette over the edge as another missile burst from the city-state's distant wall, blasting in a beautiful shower of red and yellow against the blue of the sky. Even in broad daylight, they were spectacular.

I didn't have time to enjoy the display. Breesten glued to my shoulder, I sprinted past the distracted guards and surged up the metal staircase.

"They're not bombs – perhaps they're a threat!" In my peripheral vision, I saw the biggest guard shove the others back toward the entrance to the fourth floor. "We need to send troops to the source and demand an explanation from whomever is instigating this obnoxious din!" They disappeared into the theater room, barking orders at each other, as I came to a panting halt at the top of the stairs.

Worry pumped through me like it had replaced my blood. If Zakarran troops were sent to find the source of the fireworks, Erin could be in trouble. "Wait a moment," I told Breesten as he moved down the balcony, and I pulled the texter back out. *They're coming to find out who set off the fireworks. Are you safe?*

Erin's answer appeared on my screen so quickly that I guessed she'd anticipated my message. *I'm fine. I* threw the fireworks over the wall, so they'll probably blame mischievous Zakarran teenagers. You should know by now that I'm too smart to get caught.

Reassured, I jogged over to Breesten, who had paused in front of a plain brown door. I wrenched it open – it was thankfully unlocked – and hurried through, Breesten treading on the heels of my shoes in his haste. A long passage stretched before us, more rickety than the previous three. It was long and narrow, with dust covering the wooden floor like a thin film. Obviously, King Gerald and his cohorts did not enter this level by way of the balcony very often.

"After you," I whispered to Breesten. I tried to sound unruffled, but my insides surged with pusillanimity. Fortunately, Breesten didn't seem to perceive my cowardice as he squeezed past me and led the way down the corridor, broad shoulders nearly scraping the claustrophobic walls.

He walked slowly, but I didn't urge him to hurry up. In fact, I wanted nothing more than to forget about the inevitable deed that we needed to carry out – the actual elimination of King Gerald. Despite his cruelty toward his subjects, I almost agreed with Gordon's mother; no one, no matter how heartless, deserved to be slaughtered.

But if we didn't assassinate the king, *I* would be killed. Given over for execution by my own father. To tear my mind from these haunting thoughts, I lifted the texter close to my face and sent a new message to Erin. *On the fifth floor. We should be done with the mission soon.*

This time, Erin didn't offer any advice. Her message said simply, *Good luck.*

Thanks, I typed back, trying to convey all my thoughts in that one word. I wanted to write more, like about how I was glad to have such a smart, amazing friend, and how I was grateful for all her assistance on this suicidal mission, and how even though I pretended to be annoyed by her fascination with explosives, I really admired her flair for bombs. Most of all, I yearned to tell her that if somehow this mission failed and I never returned home, I wanted her to know that she was the kindest, most cheerful, most loyal person I knew, and nothing on earth could ever replace her friendship.

But there was no time to write an essay about what I had been too foolish to tell Erin before. Before my fingers could tap out another word, we had reached the end of the passage, where yet another door indicated the entrance to the main part of the fifth floor. "Ready?" Breesten asked, preparing to shove it open.

"No," I said.

"Too bad." He wrenched the doorknob with blatant enthusiasm and swung open the door.

My first impression of the space on the other side revealed the fifth floor to be the quietest, most modest storey we'd entered yet. A simply embroidered maroon rug, not luxuriously thick or bearing some swanky design, ran down the hall like a peaceful red river, and a sprawling family tree of Zakarran royalty occupied the left-hand wall.

"Did Tomkins tell you which way to King Gerald's bedroom?" I asked Breesten.

"Yeah, a Spy found that out for him," Breesten said importantly. "We go down this hall, and it's the last door on the right." He pulled out his sword. "Remember, *I* get to actually kill him."

I shrugged to show that I had no problem with that one condition. The silence on this floor made me uneasy. I'd expected guards, alarms, some sort of opposition, but the very air felt stale, like no one had breathed it in years. I couldn't shake off the feeling that King Gerald's army lurked just around the corner, shining their swords in anticipation of an ambush.

Breesten clutched his sword in a white-knuckled grip, and I pulled out my kitchen knife and wrapped my fingers securely around it. I felt utterly exposed. For the first time, I almost wished I had a sword. Almost.

Adrenaline screeched through me with each footstep as we stole down the hall, the maroon carpet hushing our footsteps. No bells clanged, no sirens wailed, and no armed guards leapt at us from doorways. We reached the end of the hall without incident.

"So close," Breesten breathed, staring at the door to the king's bedroom. "Just think – a minute from now, I will have accomplished my first mission." His eyes shone and his breath came in quick gasps, like the excitement coursing through him required more oxygen than normal. "I feel better than I ever have in my life. Don't you?"

I didn't answer. Truthfully, I felt sicker than I could remember ever feeling before. My muscles ached like I'd just run fifteen miles, my hair stuck to my forehead and neck with nervous sweat, and my leg burned under the sword-slapped bloodstain on my pants. And on top of all that, the awful knowledge that I might soon die pounded through me with every tick of the clock.

"Let's get it over with," I whispered, voice cracking.

Breesten tried the door; it was locked, of course, but this time he already knew what to do. He stuck his blade in the crack between the door and the wall and started rasping away at the bolt. Each scrape of metal on metal sent a fresh thrill of icy terror into my chest.

Finally, the bolt fell away. Breesten and I locked eyes – his full of anticipation, mine brimming with dread. I reminded myself that there would be death behind this door. There would be pain and pleading and spurts of blood pumped from a wound by a heart's final beats, but I had to face those things. I had to stay strong. After all, if King Gerald didn't die, I would.

Summoning a shaky scrap of courage, I shouldered past Tack Breesten and pushed open the door.

The room was enormous and surprisingly uncluttered. I would have thought that King Gerald would have countless artifacts of his wealth circling his bedside – piles of silver and gold, desks crammed with the latest technology, crowns and scepters and paintings hanging from the walls – but he had chosen a simpler, more elegant décor.

A long glass window overlooked a section of his garden, giving a stunning view of exotic, orange-leafed fruit trees, fountains, and cobbled paths. A single tapestry hung above the window, depicting the serious faces of all the past Zakarran kings. At the far right of the tapestry was a picture of sad-eyed King Gerald, staring mournfully at the opposite wall.

Breesten entered the room behind me, his feet thumping heavily on the floor. I pressed a finger to my lips and pointed toward the stately bed at the opposite end of the room. It was a grand, regal piece of furniture. In fact, it looked more like a royal chariot than a bed.

"He's asleep," I whispered, pointing at a man-sized lump that huddled under the covers.

"Great!" Breesten hissed. He unsheathed his sword and grinned wickedly.

I glanced uneasily around the room, hastily easing the door shut behind us. This seemed too simple; why were there no guards? And why was King Gerald snoozing in his bed in the middle of the day when he knew that a top-notch Dominan assassin was just starving to slit his throat?

"Why is he sleeping?" I asked Breesten anxiously. "It doesn't seem right."

"Who cares?" he answered. "Your bigheaded friend Erin said herself that King Gerald is old and ill. Maybe he's too sick to get out of bed."

I nodded and drew a shaky breath. We were so close, yet the deed still had to be carried out. I gave Breesten a push toward the Zakarran king's bed. "Hurry up and get it over with."

He tiptoed up to the bed. Despite my disinclination to watch the king's life drain from his body, I followed. My feet padded silently and my breath froze somewhere between my lungs and throat; in only a few more seconds, my execution could be prevented.

Now we stood over the king's bed. He was burrowed under a purple quilt, thick yet feathery as it draped over his lumpy body. He didn't stir as we stared down at him. Breesten raised his sword and grinned at me.

"You can cover your eyes if you want," he said. He whispered the words so quietly that nearly no sound came out.

"Never," I mouthed firmly, despite the fact that before he'd mentioned it, I'd been prepared to turn the other direction and plant my hands firmly over my ears.

Still, as the muscles in his shoulders tensed and he readied himself to let the blade come plunging down, I twisted my face away and squeezed my eyes shut.

Whoosh! The blade dove downward. I expected to hear the ripping of muscles, the shredding of tissue, and the brittle splintering of frail bones, but instead the point made a soft, anti-climatic thump.

My eyes flew open. Breesten slashed his sword, ripping deep through the still body, and pulled his blade free. Something white and fluffy stuck to the razor-sharp edge as he yanked, and from the wound, from where blood should have gushed, a mound of cotton balls rolled out.

He spat on King Gerald's quilt in disgust. Then he tore back the covers to reveal the lump we had thought was the king. We stared at each other in horrible dismay as we realized that the bulge we'd thought to be the king was nothing more than a cotton-stuffed dummy.

"A hoax," Breesten breathed hoarsely. "We've been tricked."

"Yes," came a low, smooth voice from behind us. I stiffened. This voice held hatred, derisive amusement, and ruthlessness, all rolled together in a sour amalgamation and spat out in its owner's words. "I've caught you, Dominan Fighters," the voice continued as I slowly spun around. "You have failed."

Breesten and I tentatively lifted our eyes to meet the face of our foe. My mind absorbed his nasty silk suit and his cold, glistening, eyes. Then his lips crept apart into a cold alligator smile.

Head Advisor Wallace Piardak stood in the doorway, sharp teeth bared in a grin of elation that he had discovered us.

~ 11 ~

"I'll kill you!" Breesten said, words flying boldly from his mouth like Piardak would wither away from that statement alone.

Piardak wore a sword at his side, but he didn't reach for it. His alligator smile grew even wider. "I don't think so," he said coldly. "Drop your weapons!"

The knife I had shakily pulled from my belt clattered to the floor. Breesten shot me a disgusted look and clenched his sword with a renewed grip. "I'll kill you!" he threatened again. He held up the sword, brandishing it fiercely, demonstrating its power. "I will!" he said, and I didn't doubt him. "I came to kill King Gerald, but since you're on his side, I'll dispose of you as well!"

Piardak leered even more smugly. "You think you're so clever," he purred. "Domina has always held a reputation for producing arrogant, hotheaded warriors. But now the time has come for you to realize that you're not as magnificent as you've been led to suppose."

My tongue flailed clumsily in my mouth, stumbling for words. "What do you – "

"I'll show you exactly what I mean," said Piardak calmly, anticipating my question. Breesten chose this moment to lunge forward with his sword, but the smattering of guards that filled the doorway behind Piardak caused him to screech to a halt, probably creating long black skid marks on King Gerald's white marble floor.

"Drop your sword," Piardak demanded, still speaking in his calm, authoritative voice.

"No!" Breesten shouted, and he would have regained his momentum and rushed straight at the mob of guards if I hadn't shoved him in the other direction.

"The bathroom!" I shouted, pointing at the closed door at the back of the chamber. It was obvious that we held no chance of escape, but perhaps we could seek refuge in the king's bathtub until these crazed Zakarran guards grew weary of rattling the doorknob.

We bolted for the door. Even through the magnified booming of my heart, I heard shouts and running footsteps as more guards rushed down the hall to Piardak's side. Breesten reached the door first, gave the knob a firm twist, and turned to me, eyes shining with bright fireworks of panic. "Locked!" he yelled, and proceeded to spit abuses toward me that fell like misaimed missiles onto dead ears.

My mind began to shut down from fright. I spun – and saw the four guards approaching, weapons drawn. But these weapons weren't swords. They looked like the old-fashioned weapon my professor had shown me what seemed like a lifetime ago. *"Does anyone know what this is?"* he had asked.

And I'd answered. *"It's a rifle."*

One guard's finger twitched on the trigger, and I saw an impossibly fast blur plow into Breesten's chest. He staggered, reeling against the bathroom door, face twitching as though fighting off uninvited sleep.

"Linna…" he choked. Then his eyes drooped shut, and he crumpled to the floor beside me.

My mind refused to accept what my eyes could not deny – Tack was dead. I was backed against the wall, and now another guard pointed his weapon at me.

"No…" I started, twisting away, but then a sharp pain pierced my shoulder, and I felt the floor reach up to greet me. I landed in blackness before I even hit the ground.

~

I found myself lying on something hard – a concrete floor. My gaze slid up to find a gray wall rising austerely before me to match. But when I rolled onto my back, I didn't find the ceiling; instead I found myself staring at the bluest sky I'd ever seen. Across the azure expanse scudded clouds that looked as soft and sweet as cotton candy. I licked my lips. They were dry and sore and stiff, like I'd just woken from an exhausted sleep. "I'm dead," I whispered.

Someone laughed behind me. I sat straight up – sending cries of pain from my shoulder spinning through my body – and whirled around, finding myself face-to-face with a sparkle-eyed man in a color-stained apron, paintbrush twirling in his right hand and an easel heavy with paintings before him. "Hello, Linna," he said, and laughed again. His laugh sounded wonderfully familiar, like something I'd been waiting all my life to hear.

"Who are you?" I asked.

"I am an artist," the man replied, holding up his palette and brush to prove it. He motioned at the vivid sky. "Do you like my work?"

"I'm dead," I said again.

He simply laughed and shook his head.

"Okay – if I'm not dead, I'm probably in a coma, suffering irreversible brain damage, having a weird hallucination." I put a hand to my head and winced as pain whooshed through my every muscle. I must be alive – a dead person wouldn't be able to experience such severe soreness. "And you can't paint the sky," I informed the beaming artist.

He raised an eyebrow. "Really? Watch what happens when I turn the page." He bent back the current painting on his easel, and the blue sky and clouds overhead melted away to an inky blackness dazzled with stars.

I didn't know what to say, so I blurted out, "I think maybe I *am* dead."

The artist shook his head again. He set down his paintbrush and beckoned me toward him. I stiffly shoved myself to my feet and stood at his shoulder as he pointed out the constellations on his painting of the night sky. I noticed that both his hands bore ugly scars, so large and unsightly that I wondered how he managed to paint with such precision and splendor. I didn't ask how he'd received those scars; he might not want to talk about it, and my head throbbed enough already without any new information to absorb.

"This is amazing," I said, staring at the spangled canvas. I wondered how he'd made the stars so lifelike, so that they appeared to actually twinkle and glow on the page.

"I painted a picture of you," the artist said, voice astoundingly humble. "Would you like to see it?" Encouraged by my nod, he flipped through the stack of pages clipped to his easel and finally revealed an image of a dark-haired girl, trapped at the age when it was hard to tell if she was a kid still or had become an adult. The details still looked unfinished, pencil lines showing through the brush strokes, and the hair swept back into an undefined ponytail. But the pose was unmistakable. My head faced up, toward something beyond the canvas, and my mouth and eyes glowed as though captured mid-laugh.

"It's a work in progress," the artist explained. "But look – the eyes are done; I used the same color for your mother."

At the mention of my mom, my breath snagged as though grabbed by a fist. "You painted her, too?"

"I've painted everyone. I used the same color on the underpainting of your skin as I did for your dad."

I gazed into the joyful eyes of my portrait for a long time, as though I could suck some of the painting's obvious happiness into myself. Then the artist cleared his throat. "Well," he said, "you'd better get back to your mission."

Then I realized that we were not alone in the square, concrete room. Tack Breesten lay on his face a few feet away, eyes shut and thick arms strewn wide. "Is he dead?" I asked.

"No, just sleeping. He'll wake up soon. The two of you are both alive and fit to carry out what needs to be done."

"I don't want him to wake up," I said. "He's tried to kill me multiple times. He hates me. He – "

The artist silenced my protests by holding up one wounded hand. "His painting's still rougher than yours, but give him time – I'll paint him into something worth framing. Right now, you need to work with him."

"I don't want to do anything with him – I'm going to die! I don't want to die!" Fear fractured my voice as I said this. Death had hung over me so closely these last couple days, and now that I found myself locked in a concrete room with my bitterest enemy and a stranger armed with a paintbrush, somewhere in the palace where the man I'd been sent to kill resided, it didn't seem likely I'd be able to escape an early end.

"I can't finish your painting if you don't live your life, no matter how short it might be," the artist said. "Why are you scared? Give me some credit! I sculpted the mountains! I invented the colors you see each sunrise and sunset! If I can paint the stars in the sky, don't you think I have the power to save your life, should I choose?"

"Who are you?" I asked, now surer than ever that I was hallucinating.

"You know who I am."

"No – I don't – " But even as my mouth formed the denial, I couldn't help thinking that there was something familiar about the warm way he laughed, the way his scarred hands deftly twirled the paintbrush.

But suddenly the artist and his easel were gone, the starry sky was gone, and I flung open my eyes from the vivid dream and found myself lying in darkness on a cement floor in a small, square room. Five feet away, Breesten's eyelids started flickering, and his mouth began to gasp in some sort of nightmare.

I scuttled to his side and shook him. "Tack! Wake up!"

He screamed, and I stuffed both hands hard over his mouth. Then his eyes flew open. I slowly removed my hands.

"Oh. It's you, Linna." He lifted himself to a sitting position and rubbed his chest. "I thought – I thought they killed us."

I felt my shoulder, immediately remembering the twitch of the guard's finger on the trigger of his gun, the way pain had exploded through me. "I – I don't think they had bullets," I said. "It must have been some kind of dart, something to knock us out so they could lock us in here."

Breesten leapt to his feet and threw himself at the thick metal door that interrupted the gray walls of our cell. "They *did* lock us in!" he shouted, as if he couldn't believe it. He bit his lip, and shadowy, fuming creases appeared between his eyebrows the way that clouds darkened before a storm.

"We've failed!" he bellowed, directing his anger at me. "This is your fault, Nichols! I told you this would happen if I let you tag along!" He swung a fist at me, but I ducked before the blow could strike and his hand glanced off the wall instead.

"It's not my fault!" I defended myself. "Piardak and King Gerald are to blame; they're the ones who placed a dummy in the royal bed."

I could see Breesten's small, apish brain taking in this information. "True," he admitted. "But without you, I could've fought my way out!" He lowered his voice to imitate Piardak's silky drone. "Drop your weapons!"

Then he trembled and raised his voice to resemble mine. "Sure, Piardak, whatever you say!" He pantomimed dropping a knife to the ground. "You're too cowardly to attack anyone, even when your honor is at stake!"

I remembered with a sickening lurch in my stomach that more than my honor was at stake; our failed mission meant my life would be brought to an abrupt end within a day. Fighting the burning sensation that scalded the insides of my eyelids, I dug deep in my pocket. I almost swooned with relief when I felt the hard shape of my texter; the guards hadn't discovered and appropriated it, as they apparently had Breesten's sword. I whipped it out and sent a furious message to Erin.

We're caught and thrown in prison. The mission's failed. I am going to die.

I knew my words sounded melodramatic, but they were completely true and matched my morbid mood. I tried to disregard Breesten's muttered threats and insults as I stared at the screen and willed Erin to reply quickly.

No answering message appeared for what seemed like forever. Then Erin's text blinked onto the screen. *I'm sorry, Linna. Don't give up. Remember my advice.*

I battered the texter's tiny keyboard in a rush of frustration, demanding an explanation; why couldn't Erin give straightforward instructions for once, now that my situation had turned so grave? Which piece of advice did she mean? She spewed out counsel the way the sky spilled rain during a thunderstorm. It was impossible to determine what she was talking about.

An opus of hideous thumps and bangs turned my attention back to Breesten, who now flailed at the concrete wall and metal door with his fists as though he could hammer his way free. The pounding had no effect. He fell back, panting, alternating his glare between the walls of the cell and me.

What advice? My texter now read. *What am I supposed to do? How do we escape?* I pressed the button to send the message and then dropped the texter in surprise as the door suddenly burst open, causing Breesten to topple into me. Two guards, both holding guns and wearing expressions of distaste, stood in the doorway, blocking any hope of escape.

"What's that?" the taller guard demanded, pointing his weapon at the texter.

I scooped it off the ground and held it in a sweaty fist. "Nothing," I said, my voice barely loud enough to hear. "It's just – "

"Hand it over!" the shorter guard bellowed, pointing his gun at me. "Now!"

"But I – "

"Do as he says!" ordered the first guard, fixing me with a hostile glare. "If you don't obey us, we can make the rest of your miserably short lives unbearable!"

Vitriolic rage heating my blood, I tossed the texter at the guards. The shorter one caught it and stuffed it in his pocket.

I felt like something inside me had died. With the confiscation of the texter, I had lost my only link to Erin, to Domina, to the world outside these hostile palace walls.

A taller figure appeared behind the two guards. With a feeling of dread, I recognized Piardak's wickedly sharp teeth.

"Get away from me!" Breesten yelled, wrenching off his shoe and chucking it at the king's second-in-command in a fit of rage. I felt like lobbing a shoe at Piardak myself; I knew he was only doing his job, but if it wasn't for his meddling, King Gerald would be dead and we would be on our way home. But almost worse than his devastation of our mission was his patronizing alligator smile.

"Now, now," said Piardak. His tone was meant to be soothing, but it sounded more like a sinister growl. "I'm not going to hurt you. At least not yet."

Breesten and I glowered at him as he dismissed the guards and fastened a thin sheet of Plexiglas over the doorway. "Can you still hear me?" he asked. His smile was icy and mocking.

"Yes," I said angrily. "How long are you going to hold us as prisoners?"

He didn't respond; he only bared his sharp teeth in a grin that somehow made me think that we would *never* be released. "You have no doubt realized that your mission has failed," he said.

Breesten let out a howl of agony and pounded a thick fist against the wall. "You cheated!" he roared. "It was a dirty trick to place a dummy in the king's place! Let us out and give us a fair shot, or the Dominan Governor will send his entire army to slaughter you and your cruel, conniving King Gerald!"

Piardak smiled again. The insincere expression didn't reach his eyes. "Don't feel bad," he rumbled. "It was obvious that you didn't stand a chance." He sneered unpleasantly. "I relied on the Dominan Governor's obsolete sense of *honor* – "he spat the word as though it tasted like acid – "to lure you into an impossible mission."

His reptilian face lit up as though someone had draped evil Christmas lights over his bony skull. "That's the problem with Domina," he explained. "Your people are so proud, so stubborn, so devoted to honor and glory, that they expect everyone else to play by the same rules."

"It's not fair!" Breesten hollered. "I could've killed him! I could've killed the king!"

Now Piardak's expression became even more animated. Smugness and triumph danced in his eyes while arrogance flashed through his features like a bright, hideous neon sign. "No," he said deviously. "You couldn't have."

"I'm the top Fighter!" Breesten bellowed. "I *could!*"

"No," said Piardak. "I'm afraid that would have been quite unachievable. King Gerald is impossible to kill."

Despair saturated every cell in my body as he uttered his words of victory. "You see, there is no King Gerald. He died two years ago."

~ 12 ~

At words so appalling, Breesten's raging ceased. He gulped like a fish through the Plexiglas, a fish speechless before an alligator's carnivorous grin. When he spoke, it was not to Piardak. "It's your fault, Nichols," he growled.

I didn't say anything.

"Your fault," he said again, louder, spinning to face me. "If I'd come by myself, I wouldn't be stuck in this cell right now – I'd have discovered the trick and gone home to Domina in dignity!'

He whipped his head to challenge Piardak again. "You have to let me free! You made a deal with Governor Nichols; if the Fighter fails the mission, only *one* citizen loses his or her life!"

"Hey, wait a minute…" I started, but Breesten interrupted.

"Your dad was going to sacrifice you anyway – don't deny it! Erin as good as told me the day before yesterday in the Triumvirate Building. Piardak, sir, you have to let me free!"

Piardak ignored him; his beady eyes had now focused on me. "Nichols," he said softly. "I know that name. Your dad is the Governor of Domina."

I felt like his words had grabbed me with fingers like ice. A cold terror crept down my spine and chilled my limbs to shaking, even though I tried to stand unflinchingly.

"I wonder what the Governor will give to free his daughter," mused Piardak. "Imagine the ransoms he could give me! Gold, servants, technology, land…" he smirked. "And once he's paid me everything I could possibly want and sent his city-state into despair, I'll kill you publicly."

If he could have reached through the Plexiglas and stroked my cheek with his sharp, wicked fingers like a villain in a fairytale, he would have. Instead he stared into my eyes with a combination of fascination and loathing until I had to shrink toward the opposite end of the cell and tear away my gaze.

"My father will never give anything to you," I said. My voice trembled slightly, but I was pleased to find it sounded strong, even fierce.

Piardak shook his head. "He already has. As soon as you are disposed of, Domina will be mine to control. I've spoken to your father; I know what he's like. He is a man of his word; he will never back down from his promises, not even when keeping them causes him unbearable pain."

I wished my father wasn't a masochist. I wished that I had never embarked on this pointless mission in the first place. Right now I could be back in Domina attending my lessons, listening to Erin's ceaseless blabbering, and enjoying my last few hours of existence. But because I had chosen to pursue this foolhardy quest, the rest of my life would be spent listening to an alligator-like megalomaniac.

Now that Piardak had started speaking, it seemed like he couldn't stop. "Yes," he said, "King Gerald has been dead two years now. No one knows he's dead besides me – no one but his doctor, whose coffee I slyly poisoned less than an hour after the king's last breath. He had no heirs. I've been acting as king since then. It's been the height of my life. I can do whatever I want without falling in public favor, because everyone blames the king for their misfortunes; no one assumes that his Head Advisor has any control. Not even the servants have any idea that King Gerald is no more. I personally deliver his meals to his bedroom – where I eat them – and announce that he is too ill to see any visitors."

"You're repulsive," I declared. I couldn't remember ever insulting anyone like this before, and suddenly I felt a rush of boldness. I was going to die soon anyway, so what did I care if Piardak grew furious at me? "You're depraved! Narcissistic! Delusional!" All Erin's favorite insults rushed into my mind. "You're a slimy raw meatball bobbing in sewage! Gunpowder too soggy to even ignite!"

"Mean and nasty," Breesten chimed in. His vocabulary had always been somewhat unspectacular.

"Enough of this!" Piardak roared. He pointed at me. His finger was disproportionately long for his chubby hand, the nail sharp as his teeth. "You – I will personally carry out your execution at dawn, as is tradition."

I wondered what sort of city-state was so sick that there were traditional methods of murdering people.

"Goodnight to both of you," Piardak said. "Pleasant dreams."

He called to the guards, and they returned and slammed the metal door with a bang that resounded like an unending scream.

"He's going to kill me," Breesten moaned. "My very first mission, and I'm going to die!" He beat ineffectively at the door with both fists.

I didn't try to comfort him; how could I, when I couldn't even wrap my mind around the fact that I would be dead by tomorrow morning? Instead of sneaking into Zakarra, I should have hopped into the passenger's seat of Erin's car and ordered her to drive as far away from Domina as possible. It would be better to roam the wilderness as a hermit than to be exterminated by an evil man like Piardak.

"They took my sword!" Breesten wailed. "Give me back my sword! I'll kill them all! I don't want to die!"

"Piardak never said anything about killing you!" I finally snapped. "He's probably going to let you go. So stop screaming!"

Breesten abruptly ceased his inane wailing. "I wanted to succeed in my first mission," he said. "I didn't think they would resort to low-down tricks!" He stamped his foot with such force against the floor that the entire cell shuddered. "The nerve! Telling me to kill the king when there *is* no king!"

I sat down on the cold floor and wrapped my arms around my knees. "There's nothing we can do about it now," I said.

Breesten scowled; he couldn't stand feeling powerless. "Do you think your dad will save me, Linna?"

"I expect so," I said coldly. "Maybe after I'm executed he'll send in a rescue party." Sarcasm had never been one of my endowments, but suddenly my tongue felt sharp and piercing. "I'm sure that after he makes certain that I'm good and dead, he'll storm Zakarra to let you free."

I turned to face the wall and let Breesten's tantrum churn behind me. Inwardly, I seethed at my father. If not for him, I'd have happy future hopes of my existence as an octogenarian instead of dread of my imminent death. Even if my life had been destined to be short, without my father's control it could at least have been more carefree. I hadn't wanted to become a Fighter, but his dream had dominated my childhood since before I could remember. When I'd announced my chosen career barely over a year ago, I'd never even considered that I might possess the freedom to choose to be anything else.

No. That was wrong. I'd fantasized about becoming an artist – but I'd always known those were merely whimsies.

I could have chosen a different path. Dad did nothing to stop me. But I'd chosen to become a Fighter because I knew that was his desire, and I wanted to make him proud – even if that meant making myself miserable.

Erin was right. I was a masochist, just like my dad.

~

I probably would have moped in the cell for hours if the two guards hadn't reopened the door so that we could see them on the other side of the Plexiglas. The first one held the texter in his hand and lifted it to the pane so that I could see.

"Can I have it back?" I asked hopefully. Maybe they would be merciful toward a prisoner doomed to die so soon. Was it possible that they, like the servants and the kitchen workers, were disloyal toward the nonexistent King Gerald?

"Of course not," the guard scoffed, and my hopes plummeted several miles. "With whom are you communicating? What have you told him?"

"None of your business," Breesten cut in. "Either give back the texter or leave us alone."

The guard prodded the texter's screen, relishing the sight of my discomfort. "Hey, look!" he said, grinning at his companion. "You have a message!"

My whole body grew heated with rage; I felt like I could combust, shattering the barrier between our cell and the guards. "Give it back," I demanded, aware that my words were feeble and only invigorated their enjoyment.

"Looks like someone's worried about you," the guard taunted, squinting at the words on the screen. He twisted his voice to a mocking whine. "*It's been hours. Are you okay?*' I'd better reassure your friend on the other end that everything's fine."

My fury slowly sizzled and cooled as I realized that Erin already knew the mission had failed. If the guards sent her a message saying that we were all right, she would know that an impostor had taken hold of the texter. But what use would that knowledge be if we remained locked in this cell and she lingered somewhere outside of Zakarra?

"What should I write?" the guard asked aloud. His eyes fixed on me again. "What's your friend's name, prisoner?"

I pressed my lips together and refused to answer. His eyes bored into mine like two dark, endless pits. I felt like if I stared into them too long, I would fall into his pupils and be sucked down a narrow tunnel to my death.

"Answer him!" the other guard barked, slapping the Plexiglas with a meaty fist.

"Phil," I lied, saying the first name that popped into my head.

The first guard shook his head in disgust. "She's lying. Never mind, I don't need to use a name." He began to tap at the tiny letters with his oversized fingers, mouth pursed in concentration.

After a minute of clicking keys, he held up the texter. "There!" he declared. "It says: *Everything is fine. The mission will be over soon. I'll tell you once the king is dead.*"

One jab of his fleshy thumb sent the message on its way. I stared at the texter's screen, trying to send Erin a message of my own telepathically, but I knew it was no use. Even if she was aware of my predicament, it would take something much more miraculous than her prodigious Strategist's mind to get me out of here alive.

Suddenly, the guard jerked.

"What's wrong?" grunted his friend.

The first guard brought the texter to his ear and squinted. "It's making a funny noise. Do you hear that?"

I held my breath and realized that I could hear a faint humming, increasing to a pitch so alarming that the guard dropped the texter and backed away, leaving it to clatter on the linoleum floor of the hall.

The other guard leaned over the texter. "There's a message!" he said, "It says, *Back away from this texter, you nauseating reprobate, or say farewell to your eyebrows!*"

The thugs wasted no time backpedaling frantically, scrambling to the end of the hall and then hugging the wall, eyes glued to the still humming device. Immediately I realized what Erin had done, and I missed her more than ever.

The humming stopped. A split second later, the texter detonated with a booming flame and a cloud of orange smoke, half-melted shards of metal and plastic flying across the floor. A few pieces shot into the Plexiglas over the doorway, making Breesten and me tumble against the back wall of the cell in surprise.

When the smoke cleared, the texter had vanished, diminished to a layer of smoldering dust. The guards had escaped the worst of the damage, but their skin was blackened by soot and, as Erin had predicted, their eyebrows were burnt off.

"You'll pay!" a guard shouted through sooty lips, glaring at Breesten and me like he wanted to slice us to shreds with his eyes. "I hope your execution is as painful as possible!" With that, he and his companion scuttled down the hall and rushed away, leaving the texter's remains on the floor.

~ 13 ~

The remainder of the night seemed to crawl by sluggishly. Although I'd thought that I'd want to appreciate every last second of life, in truth it was almost a relief when two new guards arrived at the cell door to escort Breesten and me to our execution. Trepidation had chased sleep from my body the entire night, and suddenly I wanted my death to arrive as quickly as possible, before I had to endure any more dread.

"You get one last meal," said one of the guards, twirling his dark mustache. "Then – " he didn't complete his sentence, but instead drew a finger across his throat and cackled at our pallid complexions.

I created desperate scenarios in my mind. Breesten and I were two well-trained Fighters – Dominan Fighters, the best in the world. Would we be able to overpower the guards when they tried to drag us from this cell?

I wanted to communicate with Breesten, but the guards tracked every twitch of my fingers or tilt of my head. Telepathy had never sounded so appealing; I tried to send waves of nonverbal messages, but I doubted that any of them penetrated Breesten's thick, gorilla-like skull.

Our last meal turned out to be cold red soup. I had a nasty suspicion that this was the soup that the kitchen worker had spat into, so I only picked at my bowl. I hadn't thought that hunger would taunt me so close to my doom, but it clawed at my insides like an animal frantic to escape.

"Eat it," Breesten told me, shoveling the liquid down his throat.

"But that girl – "

"Who cares?" he said. "Piardak ate it, and he hasn't keeled over yet."

I decided that, for once in his life, Breesten had a point. I dripped the cold soup into my mouth and tried not to think about the pathogens that could potentially be sliding into my stomach with every spoonful. I would be dead before the bacteria could harm me, anyway.

Remembering the girl who had helped us enter the palace made me wonder if the guards knew she had offered us her assistance. I turned toward the Plexiglas and asked, "How did you figure out that we were in King Gerald's bedroom?"

The man with the mustache curled his mouth into a sneer, his facial hair performing a pompous jig. "You ignoramuses set off Piardak's alarm. What sort of dimwitted fools stop for a snack during an assassination attempt? Then Rudolph – my coworker – found an apron at the bottom of the staircase. It didn't take much brainpower to realize that you'd sneaked in through the kitchen."

I gritted my teeth and hoped fruitlessly that our collaborators in the kitchen had managed to dodge punishment.

The guard's mustache jiggled gleefully. "We interrogated the kitchen workers; they admitted their contribution to your mission. Every one of them has been lashed with a barbed whip and deprived of pay for a month."

Guilt washed over me like a tsunami wave, drenching my insides and clogging my lungs. Angry words gurgled in my throat, begging to spring off my tongue and through my lips, but I satisfied myself with shooting a glare like a deadly laser through the Plexiglas. Even Breesten appeared scandalized by this harsh punishment. "They were whipped just because they let us into the palace?" he asked.

"You were prepared to murder them with your sword, Tack," I reminded him. "A few gashes and a month of slave labor pales in comparison with death."

The guard's entire face brightened. "Speaking of death," he said conversationally, "have you finished your soup? Because I'm supposed to escort you to the roof for your execution."

His silent partner stepped forward, and the two of them pushed away the Plexiglas. Breesten's hand automatically reached beneath his jacket, but it emerged empty. His crushed expression illustrated his dismay at the reminder that his sword had been confiscated.

I tried to dodge between the two guards, but the mustached man shot out an arm and blocked my escape. Then two hands curled around my wrists; his fingers felt like they were made of diamond – the grip was unbreakable.

Breesten put up a more impressive fight. His right fist shot out – *wham!* – and connected with the second guard's chest. The guard staggered back a couple of steps, but he must have donned a protective vest beneath his uniform because he immediately regained his balance and pulled out his tranquilizer gun.

"I'll shoot if you don't let me handcuff you," he said.

I felt slightly offended that they didn't think I was a big enough threat to bother to shackle me too.

My mind screamed that now, if ever, was the time to fight. As the guard released one of my arms to assist his friend in restraining the viciously struggling Breesten, I realized that this might prove my only chance to get away. But I hesitated. The guard could aim his gun in half a blink – even though I knew there was only a dart inside, not a bullet, all that I had heard about those brutal ancient weapons caused my bones to ring with fear.

I wavered too long; together the guards snapped the cold rings around Breesten's wrists and then the mustached one renewed his grip on me. Everything inside me seemed to sink as I realized I'd just lost my only chance.

Breesten continued to wrench and resist, but the handcuffs had rendered flight unattainable. He let his feet scrape along the floor of the passage as the guards led us out of the cell, but I trudged along obediently. My thoughts, however, churned so fast that I couldn't keep track of them. The thumping of our footsteps rang too loudly in my ears. My body was superbly aware of every breath and heartbeat. Though my feet shuffled forward like they belonged to an automaton, I had never before felt so conscious of the act of living.

It seemed an eternity ago that I'd bantered with Erin about her driving or shuddered whenever Phil Falconer came near. The test we'd taken three – or had it now been four? – days ago seemed like a tiny blip on the radar of life. I never would have seethed over Falconer's cheating if I'd known that I would be cheated of something far greater in such a short amount of time – my life.

"Please," Breesten begged, resorting to good manners. "Please!"

"Quit your sniveling," the mustached guard barked. "No mercy has ever been shown to whiners."

Breesten scowled to show that his eyes were dry and added a tough growl to his voice. "Let me free this instant or you'll have the Governor of Domina to answer to!"

The guard snickered. "Oh, yes," he said sarcastically. "I'm sure that the Governor will be able to offer you plenty of help once you're dead. If he hasn't saved you by now, he's never going to."

A cold stone landed in my heart and weighed me down. I didn't know why I felt such bitter disappointment as my limbs turned heavy and abandonment flowed through me, carried by my veins and capillaries to every organ of my body. It should have been obvious that Dad wasn't going to rescue me. I doubted he even knew where I was, and intervening in Piardak's plan would be a blow to his honor.

My father had always valued honor. It shouldn't have come as a surprise that he cherished his pride more than his only daughter.

"Linna!" Breesten began to babble now. "Tell them that only one person is supposed to die! This is a mistake! Your dad and the king made a deal!"

"He's right!" I cried to the guard. "You can't execute us without the Governor's consent!" If Piardak contacted my dad, perhaps my father would insist that since Piardak had dealt dishonestly by pretending King

Gerald was alive, Domina's Governor didn't have to fulfill his part of the deal. Maybe I wouldn't be executed after all.

"No more talking!" the guard commanded, crushing my feeble prospect of survival. He and his partner began leading us up a narrow stone staircase. There were intricate patterns carved into the stone; some of them depicted beautiful flowers or scenic landscapes, but a few of them showed more lurid scenes. I stared at my shoes to avoid images of screaming men and women being burned at the stake, beheaded, or run through with metal spears. Despite my attempts to block the imminent execution from my brain, I couldn't help but wonder how my death would be carried out.

My thoughts wandered back to the absurd dream I'd had under the influence of the tranquilizer's dart. The painter's words came back to haunt me: *"If I can paint the stars in the sky, don't you think I have the power to save your life, should I choose?"*

Who was the mysterious painter? I mentally slapped myself back into reality; he was only a figment of my imagination, a character in a dream. The fortuneteller's message seemed much more real. Deeper despair than any I had ever known filled my body like water in a drowning person's lungs as I recalled her lingering words: *"You are doomed to die!"*

It seemed as if she, not the artist, had been correct.

I was going to die.

Mentally, I cursed mortality.

A thick door blocked the top of the staircase. Several bolts held the metal to the frame. The guard with the mustache abandoned his grip on one of my wrists to slide the bolts away.

Now! I jerked backwards with all my strength, nearly tumbling back down the staircase. His fingers slipped, his grip loosened, and I wrenched myself free of his hold. It took a second to regain my balance, and then I bounded down the stairs, the tantalizing tune of freedom tumbling through my mind.

"Freeze!" the guard shouted. His footfalls shot behind mine, creating a rapid percussion that elevated my heartbeats and added anxiety to the chase; the alarm pinching my throat painfully reminded me that this was no mere game of tag.

I had always been a fast runner, but even a Fighter's training had not made me capable of out sprinting a well-trained guard ten years my senior and in prime fitness. He grabbed the back of my shirt collar just as I reached the bottom of the staircase, whipping my feet out from beneath me.

I twisted – I could nearly taste emancipation – but before I could shake off his grip he'd pulled a pair of handcuffs from his pocket and forced them around my wrists.

I fought back the fire in my throat – the telltale prelude to tears – as the two guards marched Breesten and me through the door at the top of the stairs. We emerged onto the palace roof, five stories high and painted gray by pale dawn emerging in the east. The guards snapped off our manacles and took positions before the door. With our only exit blocked and a fatal drop on each side, there was no way to escape.

I spun in a full circle, trying to find some hope of avoiding death, but saw nothing besides Piardak's sharp grin as he approached from the west corner of the building. He held a sword in his right hand, the blade longer than Breesten's. As soon as I saw that sword, my heart froze in my chest and I couldn't tear my eyes away.

"He's going to *stab* us!" Breesten gasped, unable to comprehend the injustice of the situation. "With a *sword!*" That his weapon of choice should deliver the fatal blow to his body must have seemed the ultimate iniquity in his pebble-sized brain. He had yearned all his life to learn to pierce others with his blade, and now an ironic twist of circumstances had placed him at the point of his favorite weapon.

"Yes," said Piardak. "Normally my executioner would carry out the sentence, but today, I thought I'd do the deeds myself. You, sir, will be first."

"No!" Breesten yelled. "I don't want to die! I'm not supposed to die!" He shoved me in front of him, his hands cold enough to chill me even through my jacket. "She's the one you're supposed to kill – kill her! Kill Linna!"

Piardak looked me in the eyes. "I will kill you last, Linna Nichols," he said, "because I want you to watch this young man die."

I felt Breesten shaking behind me and realized that I was trembling, too. I'd hated Breesten for years; he'd picked me as his rival and had always fought to prove himself superior, and he'd tried to kill me several times in just the last two days. But I'd known him almost all my life – as long as I'd known Erin. I didn't want to see him gored on Piardak's sword.

"I won't watch," I said brashly. "I'll close my eyes."

Piardak's gaze narrowed, but he didn't object. "It doesn't matter," he said. "You'll both be dead soon, anyway." His stare snapped up to Breesten. "You," he barked, "come here."

I couldn't bear to watch Breesten struggle and shout; I turned away and moved on quavering legs to the edge of the roof, staring at the glow above the craggy mountains beyond Zakarra's walls. Breesten's footsteps and ragged breathing neared me as he backed away from Piardak, whom I heard advancing with heavy footsteps. Breesten's back brushed mine, heaving with terrified sobs. "No… no…" he blubbered.

I felt him tense as Piardak stopped in front of him. I couldn't move. My legs felt like ice. A picture of Piardak's flashing sword played over and over in my mind.

"Please!" Breesten begged tearfully. "Please…don't…"

I imagined the painter in my dream painting the shining dawn. I imagined him sketching me as a tiny silhouette on the palace roof, with Breesten at my back and Piardak raising the sword to strike. I wanted to believe what he'd said, that he could save my life. I wanted to accept that he could erase my impending death and fill me with the inexplicable joy I'd seen on my own face in his unfinished painting. So now, with death only seconds away, I decided to believe that the artist was real.

I heard nothing but a helicopter's thrum in the distance and Breesten's panting as he beheld the sword that would penetrate his heart. Piardak had hesitated too long. Cautiously, expecting to see his blade whip out at any second, I turned to see what was wrong.

Wallace Piardak, sword still high, had turned his head to the sky. His eyes tracked an approaching helicopter – no, *two* approaching helicopters, which appeared to be headed directly toward the palace.

"Those aren't Zakarran helicopters!" one of the guards yelled, flinging up his arms as though to shield himself from the sight. "Mr. Piardak – sir – I think we're under attack!"

"Don't be ridiculous!" Piardak snapped. "Those wimpy choppers are too small to carry any weapons. They would snap under the weight of a bomb powerful enough to cause any damage." He spoke with authoritative confidence, though his eyes remained fixed on the aircrafts. "Besides, they can't possibly be headed here."

His assurance evaporated when the two helicopters began their descent. Piardak's eyes widened as they touched down in the middle of the city-state's forum, no more than half a kilometer from the palace gates.

"Sir, is it Domina?" a guard cried.

Piardak didn't answer. He turned back to Breesten and me, his grip tightening on his sword. "Someone might have come to rescue you," he said in a voice so low that my ears prickled at the sound, "but it doesn't matter. You'll be dead before they make it to the palace. And with you two dead, no one will ever learn that there is no King Gerald."

"You!" Piardak pointed at Breesten. "Stand in front of the girl. Don't refuse me; if you delay to try to give your allies a chance to free you, I guarantee that your death will be much more painful. They will never arrive in time to save your life."

Breesten shook his head, but one of the guards thrust him forward with a shove. He stood in front of me, blocking my view of Piardak. I remembered my vow not to watch his execution and turned my back, squeezing my eyes shut.

Remember my advice, Erin's text had said. But it was too late for advice. And Erin had given me so many instructions over the years I'd known her that it was impossible to deduce which particular tidbit she'd had in mind.

The fortuneteller's words rang in my ears like a nasty, never-ending round, taking up all the space in my mind. Somehow, I knew without looking that Piardak had raised his sword again. Breesten's back against my own stiffened. Numbly, I realized that if Piardak drove the sword through Breesten now, the blade would pass through both of us.

"If for some reason you find yourself on the roof of the palace in a life or death situation, jump off the east side." Erin's words exploded in my head with the force of one of her beloved bombs, sending shattered fragments of the fortuneteller's prediction flying into oblivion.

In a split second, I made my decision. Erin's advice had paid off so far; even though suicide did not appeal to me, perhaps she was telling me that it was better to surrender my own life than to let a lunatic with a sword steal it from me. One final thought entered my mind before I threw myself into action: *Maybe this last act will make my dad proud.*

My right arm flew out behind me, wrapped around Breesten, and pinned him to my back. I would take him with me – even if he'd been my lifelong nemesis, I knew he'd prefer a five-storey drop to the indignity of execution. I jerked forward, straining every muscle in my body, and he toppled over my head the same way the fortuneteller had into empty space beyond, sending me down with him.

There must have still been a murderous fire in Breesten's heart, because as we plummeted off the edge of the roof, he reached out a meaty hand, determination shining in his eyes, and grabbed the astonished Piardak's sleeve. Breesten yelled, his last moment bittersweet with victory, as the shrieking Piardak joined our mortal freefall.

Even with my eyes screwed shut, death expanded unavoidably in my vision. *"Trust me,"* Erin always said. *"Trust me; I have an infallible plan."* But it seemed that she had overestimated her brilliance one too many times, because –

Splash! The impact knocked all air from my lungs, which was unfortunate considering I'd landed in deep water. I was too shocked to register what had happened – I was supposed to be *dead,* not floundering at the bottom of a swimming pool. Eyes stinging and limbs thrashing against Breesten and Piardak, I sank for what felt like forever and tried to shove off the spongy bottom. But then something heavy forced me down – Piardak had grabbed my legs, sword clutched in his fingers, and had shoved me so that my shoulder pressed into the pool floor.

My vision swam under the weight of all the water above me. I needed to get to the surface. I needed to *breathe.* Piardak raised his sword, every movement in slow motion. Underwater, his cold-blooded smile didn't remind me so much of an alligator – he looked more like a shark.

He plunged the sword down. I twisted away, but the cold metal still sliced my shoulder. Pain erupted bright red and clouded the water around me. Piardak kicked off from the bottom and swam toward the surface. I tried to follow, but the sword had pinned me by my shirt collar to the bottom of the pool.

Bubbles burst from my nose as panic tightened its grip around my heart. It took all my effort to order myself to remain calm; the cut in my shoulder was merely a scratch, though it blazed with pain like fire in the chemicals in the water. The real problem was that the sword prevented me from rising to the surface for air.

I twisted and wrenched, but freedom evaded my efforts. I reached behind me with one arm and tried to grasp the hilt, but the unnatural position allowed me little leverage and my oxygen-deprived muscles would not force the blade free.

I concluded that now would be an opportune time to submit to panic.

Piardak and Breesten had reached the surface of the pool. My eyes stung under the water, but I could make out their kicking legs as they propelled themselves to opposite sides of the pool. Neither of them re-submerged to come to my aid, and why should they? Piardak had been about to kill me anyway, and Breesten was so self-centered that thoughts of my safety had probably never even entered his minuscule skull.

Help! Help me, you selfish gorilla! I saved your life. Why won't you help me?

Now every cell in my body screamed for air. I yanked myself upward, only to jerk back down due to the sword caught in my shirt. Breesten's legs disappeared from the water, and Piardak's followed a second later.

I closed my eyes, lungs imploding. I couldn't struggle any more. I was going to drown. I was going to die.

Then, with a wrench, the blade pulled free. A determined hand closed around mine. My shoulder stung even more as someone hauled me to the surface. My head broke the water, and I opened my mouth and eyes to air and blinding light. I tried to paddle forward, feeling for the edge of the pool, but all I could do was cough and gasp. The hand around my wrist guided me to the edge, and I hugged it like a long lost friend.

Weakly, I turned to face my rescuer.

"Good morning, friend," beamed Erin.

~ 14 ~

Later Erin would fill me in on everything that had happened after her last text to me. She'd remained in the car in the woods for hours, growing increasingly anxious as she waited for news. When the guard had replied instead of me, insisting everything was fine, she knew the texter had been confiscated. She confessed to feeling malicious pleasure in activating the bomb to blow up the device in the guard's face.

Then she'd texted Phil Falconer.

Phil had rushed across Domina and banged on my door to have it flung open by my frantic father. I should have been home hours ago. A chat with Professor James Scurius revealed that I hadn't been in class again. When he contacted Erin's parents, they told him they hadn't seen either of us all day.

"Governor Nichols," Falconer had gasped, "Linna's in trouble." Falconer handed his texter to my dad, and a taut conversation with Erin outlined my situation. Meanwhile, Erin sped back toward Domina at double the speed limit – illegally texting, driving, and strategizing simultaneously on a road lacking streetlights. It was a wonder she arrived alive.

I had informed Erin that I was going to die. Assuming I had not resorted to melodramatics, Erin deduced that Breesten and I had been condemned to

179

execution – a sentence that went against the terms of the challenge agreed upon by my dad and the supposed King Gerald. After contacting Perceval Tomkins, Dad and Erin grudgingly agreed that they couldn't do anything to save us that night. Zakarra's gates had closed, and bringing a helicopter over the walls would only incite the Zakarrans to attack. Traditionally, executions in Zakarra occurred at dawn on the roof of the palace. The best time to rescue us would be while we were virtually unguarded, exposed to the open air.

Unfortunately, the helicopters landed in Zakarra's forum five minutes later than planned.

Dad, Erin, Falconer, Breesten, and the two helicopter pilots sprinted the half-kilometer to the palace at a speed that would've turned even fast-footed Breesten apoplectic with envy. Erin demolished a section of the artful mosaic wall with a hurled bomb, and they rushed through the clearing smoke and into the palace's east courtyard just in time to see Piardak, Breesten, and me plunge into the magnificent palace pool.

My dad moaned as he saw the water cloud with blood.

When Piardak and Breesten had emerged from the water and I hadn't, Phil had begun to tear off his shoes screaming, "I'll save her!"

Erin shoved him out of the way. "No, *I* will," she said fiercely, and she leapt into the pool.

But I didn't know any of this as I spat stale pool water from my mouth and took several gasps of precious air. I blinked liquid from my eyes and squinted in the sudden brightness; Breesten chased Piardak around the garden, waving a sword that he must have snatched from my father. Erin beamed at me. "You remembered my advice!" she said. "I told you that my plans were infallible!" Her grin was so wide that it threatened to pop her face like an overfilled balloon.

I managed a grateful smile. I dragged myself from the water and sprawled on my back on the grass, coughing, blinking at the lightening sky, relishing every aching breath. If I hadn't been throbbing all over, I would've shouted with elation. I was alive.

Dad rushed to my side. "Linna," he said, almost sounding concerned, "your sleeve's bloody."

I sat up and examined my shirtsleeve. The sword had ripped the material to shreds, and the area around my scratched shoulder was stained pink from water-diluted blood.

Dad's voice turned back to its usual stern tone. "I don't know what you were thinking… "

But he never got to finish his sentence because I clenched my hand into a fist like rock and punched him in the face. Erin's delighted expression as my dad's nose trickled blood through his surprised fingers evaporated any guilt I might have had.

"That's for almost letting me get executed," I said.

Dad took his hands from his nose. Shock dominated every line on his face. "I… "

I picked up a pebble from the ground and hurled it at him. It bounced harmlessly off his chest, but he still fell back on his heels in surprise. Erin's glee skyrocketed to uncontainable laughter.

"That's for everything else," I snarled at Dad. "For not telling me about Mom sooner. For raising me to be a Fighter. For turning me into *you*."

Dad didn't say anything, but the hurt in his eyes was so piercing that I felt like I had to get away. "By the way," I told him, "the king is dead. He's been dead for two years." Ignoring Dad's satisfyingly shocked expression, I scrambled to my feet and retreated with Erin along the edge of the pool. We stopped at the other end.

Erin was still laughing. "I can't believe it! You actually *punched* him! *You* did!"

I grinned. Through my anger at my father, I felt a stab of guilt for punching him, but I was so thankful to be alive, so glad to see my best friend's face after hours of thinking I'd never again behold her smile, that I forced myself to shove the guilt aside and enjoy the moment.

"Please! No!" The shriek spun my attention to Piardak, who stood quavering with his back against the courtyard wall. He'd been pressed there for the last few minutes as Breesten swung a sword in front of his face and thundered at him, but now Breesten had pressed the sword against the drenched Head Advisor's chest.

Falconer stood at Breesten's side, nodding ingratiatingly to everything his friend said.

"I'm going to kill you!" Breesten told Piardak, voice rising to a roar clearly audible even from my position across the pool. "You tried to kill me; now you can see how you like it!"

"You can't do that," Piardak gibbered. "I'm the king's second-in-command! I'm his Head Advisor!"

"King Gerald's dead," Breesten growled. "As you soon will be!"

He clenched his face and prepared to make the final thrust, neck muscles bulging with effort and hate. I wanted to shout, to turn away, but my eyes had locked on Piardak's petrified face. Even after everything he'd done, I didn't want him to die like Gordon. Gordon's mother had been right: no man deserved to be murdered, no matter how evil he might be.

"Breesten!" Dad's strict voice flew out like an icy comet, freezing Breesten mid-lunge. "What do you think you're doing?"

"Disposing of this miscreant, sir!"

Dad covered the distance between him and Breesten in a few long strides. The two were the same height, but Dad looked taller as he focused Breesten under his intimidating gaze. "Tell me, Tack, did you have orders to dispose of him?"

Piardak's legs started to tremble as he realized his fate was being decided.

"I had orders to kill the king. But there is no king, so I'm going to dispose of this lying, self-centered…"

"You had no orders to kill him," Dad said, answering his own question. He grabbed the sword from Breesten's hand and kept it leveled at Piardak's chest. "You will be taken into Dominan custody and forced to apologize to your city-state this evening for your miserable deception and for the hundreds of unjust executions performed at your commands. After that, you will remain in Domina's prison until tried, and I will find a more suitable leader to inherit King Gerald's throne."

"But sir – " Breesten protested, but Dad silenced him with a stern glance.

"Escort Mr. Piardak to the helicopter and secure him with handcuffs. Make sure he can't escape."

Breesten nodded, obviously dissatisfied. "Yes, sir," he muttered, grabbing Piardak roughly by the wrists and hauling him toward the aircraft.

"You can't do this to me, Neil!" Piardak yelled, wrenching in Breesten's rough grasp to face my father.

"You have no right to arrest me! The Governor of Domina has no right to get involved in Zakarran affairs!"

"The Zakarran Head Advisor has no right to execute two Dominan Fighters," Dad said coldly.

As much as Piardak struggled, he was no match for Breesten's muscle, and his threats faded as Breesten dragged him through the hole in the wall.

After Piardak had been taken care of, Breesten and my dad spoke in low voices. Breesten must have told him about the two dead guards at the back entrance, because Dad ordered the helicopter pilots to bring their bodies into the palace to see if any of the servants could identify them. All the chocolate and music and laughter in the world could not have diminished the aching shame that wrung my heart as Gordon's mother, catching sight of her son's still body, released a wail that shook the palace walls from the inside out.

"I don't want to be a Fighter anymore," I muttered to Erin, trying to block out the sounds of grief that echoed from the palace.

"Then don't be," Erin said.

I wished that life worked as simply as Erin's words implied.

She broke away from me. "Where are you going?" I asked.

Something mischievous danced in her eyes. "I'm going to go see how your dad liked my cookies."

I followed her with my eyes as she jogged across the garden, taking care to dent the pristine lawns with footprints. She didn't care that she was soaking wet. Not even the bulkiest complications could dampen her optimism; if something got in her way, she just blew it up. I wished I could be more like Erin, with a plan for everything.

Erin slowed in front of my father. Her words carried over the garden. "Governor Nichols, were the cookies I baked you delicious?"

My dad's voice was lower and quieter than hers, so I couldn't hear his reply from where I sat.

Erin started walking across the courtyard, arms waving emphatically, my father at her side. I could still hear her voice, but I couldn't make out the words. I fixed my eyes on Dad. His back was straight as always, but now his head tipped slightly to one side in a way I recognized as thoughtful. Erin said something else, and suddenly Dad whirled on her. Lovely – Dad would probably disown me after I'd punched him and screamed at him, and now he looked ready to strangle my best friend as well.

Erin kept talking – that was something she excelled at – and I watched in awe as Dad's rage subsided. Curiosity overtaking my resentment at my father, I sprinted across the yard to join them.

"The trick is to beat the butter and brown sugar together very smoothly before you add the other ingredients," Erin explained as my dad listened raptly. "And don't forget the vanilla – it complements white chocolate magnificently. Oh, hello, Linna," she said, catching my eye. "I was just telling your dad not to worry – you won't abandon all your Fighter education for another profession."

"But I don't want to be a Fighter," I said in frustration. Had Erin misunderstood what we'd just discussed? I spun to face my dad. "I'm not going to spend my life learning to kill people just to please you!"

Dad acted like he hadn't heard my outburst, face grave as usual. "Linna," he said, "remember two nights ago, when I told you that I'd tried to squash your mom's personality out of you? When I told you that I'd tried to make you like me? I told you that I'd succeeded."

I remembered all too clearly; the memory of his words still sent a knifelike pang slicing upward through my intestines to my heart. He must have seen the recollection on my face, because he continued. "I was wrong. If you were like me... well, for one thing, you wouldn't have a friend like Erin – " Erin grinned smugly – "and you never would have come to Zakarra to try to save your own life. You showed initiative. You made your own choices instead of obeying unfair orders, like I would have, even if it killed me. And Tack Breesten informed me – disgustedly, of course – that you prevented him from murdering people that stood in your way on many occasions."

I couldn't tell Dad's emotions from his voice. Assuming that he even had emotions.

"I would have killed them," Dad said. "That would have been the easy thing to do. But you spared their lives because your conscience protested their deaths, even though it made your own path more difficult." His voice shriveled. "You're not like me, Linna. I'm glad you're not."

All I could do was stare at him. Dad had never given a speech like this before; the only speeches I'd ever heard him utter were political ones or harsh lectures. Hearing these words from his lips, I felt like my mind had gone catatonic. I didn't know how to react. So I said and did nothing as Dad took a breath.

"You don't have to continue your Fighter training if you don't want to," he said. "It's your choice."

I thought about the blood I'd seen the last few days. I'd seen Gordon and another guard slumped over each other after Breesten stole their lives, and I'd seen Breesten plow a sword down into what I thought was a sleeping figure. I'd found myself at the point of his sword, certain he was about to impale me. I'd felt the pounding rush of fear and adrenaline pumping a frantic duet through my veins as I ran for my life.

If I weren't a Fighter, what would I be? That was a question I'd never dared consider too seriously. The image of the painter from my dream flitted into my mind. No matter what my career, I knew I'd always wonder about him. I'd go to sleep each night wondering if he might visit me again and tell me more about himself. A multitude of possibilities swam through my head like a school of splashing fish.

But through the churning prospects, all I could see was Dad's face.

I'd make a good Fighter. I'd trained all my life for it. Domina hadn't fought a battle since the Battle of the Hills fifteen years ago, so there was a chance I wouldn't see true combat within my career. My choice now was the same as it had been the first time. I wanted to make Dad proud. But if that aspiration ever required killing people, there I would draw the line.

"I'll continue," I said with a dry throat, trying to ignore the haughty smile that meant Erin had accurately predicted my decision.

Without warning, Dad wrapped his arms around me and swept me against his chest. My first thought was, *It's an attack!* My muscles tensed, ready to fight back, but then I realized my father wasn't trying to crush my ribs. This was a hug – an actual hug – and to my astonishment, I felt myself hugging Dad back.

"I'm proud of you, Linna," Dad said. "And I love you."

Then my mouth formed the words I couldn't remember ever saying before in my life. "I love you too, Dad."

In the window under my father's arm, I saw Erin's grin threaten to crack her face. And beyond her, wind ruffling his splattered apron, I saw the painter shoot me a jubilant thumbs-up. But as soon as I blinked, he was gone.

Even after Dad released me and went to prepare the helicopter pilots for our journey back to Domina, my whole body tingled with the knowledge that I'd made him proud. I felt like nothing could crush my euphoria, not even Phil Falconer with his gangly limbs, taped glasses, and gawky smile, detaching himself from Breesten and striding toward us from across the courtyard.

"Hi, Phil," I said.

He gave me a glance. "Hello." Then he turned to my friend. "Hi, Erin."

"Thanks for being our lifeline in Domina," Erin told him. "It grieves me to admit this, but without your help, Tack and Linna would probably be dead right now."

"Yeah," said Phil, "I was pretty awesome. That's me – a guy you can count on." If possible, his grin turned even more awkward. "That was impressive, the way you jumped in after Linna," he said to Erin. "You acted faster than *me*, even, and I'm really fast."

Erin and I exchanged a look, and she rolled her eyes. "Yeah, Phil, I know I'm amazing," she said. "Why don't you go mollify your gorilla friend over there; he looks pretty disappointed that he didn't get to lop off Piardak's head."

Falconer almost tripped in his hurry to get back to Breesten, who was cantankerously shredding each blossom in a flowerbed.

I watched him go. "Hey, Erin," I said, "I think Phil might be in love with *you* now."

I turned to her to see that she was fuming. "I'll soon put a stop to that," she declared. "I'm thinking of a plan that involves a sledgehammer. Do you have one I could borrow?"

After assuring her that she could borrow anything she liked as long as she didn't name me as a coconspirator in her crazy plans when she was arrested someday, we sat side by side on the immaculately manicured grass and watched the sunrise through the hole Erin had blown in the palace wall. On the palace's east side, the land dropped away in a hill with a jumble of buildings below, so we had a spectacular view. Daybreak spread orange and pink across the horizon over the disorganized, tumbledown city-state of Zakarra. It was by far the most beautiful thing I'd ever seen, especially when I remembered that I almost hadn't lived to see the dawn of this new day.

The stain of sunrise, smooth as watercolors, made me think of the painter. Now, with no death hanging over me, reason told me that he had been merely a hallucination. Some drug in the dart that had knocked me out must have produced crazy dreams, and I'd probably just imagined him behind Erin as I hugged my dad. But he'd definitely looked real. For some reason I couldn't shake him from my thoughts.

"Erin?" I said.

"Yeah?"

"Do you think someone made all this?"

She looked at me. "All what?"

"All this – the sunrise. The world. Me. You."

"Well, yeah," Erin tapped her head. "You think brains like mine just waltzed from the goop? *Of course* someone designed it all."

I sat in silence for another moment, watching the first sliver of sun glitter like a line of gold on the mountains. "I know I'm going to die someday," I said. It felt strange to admit that after days of trying to avoid my demise. "Everyone is. It's called mortality. But do you think – maybe – if someone was powerful and good enough to create all this, that that person could also come up with a way to rescue us from death?"

It sounded ridiculous, but Erin didn't laugh; for once, she thought before she talked. I could feel her beside me, just as cold and wet as I was, chewing a lock of hair, remarkable mind working. "If someone did," she finally said, "that would be the greatest plan ever."

About the Authors

Anna Trujillo lives in Anchorage, Alaska, where she will graduate from Grace Christian School in 2013. In her free time she participates in running, cross-country skiing, zombie exterminating, drawing, and eating impressive quantities of vegetables and cookies. She enjoys Chopin and Debussy and is also an awe-filled fan of sunrises and sunsets. *To Kill a King* is her first published novel, and she hopes many more will follow.

Claire Trujillo is also a part of the Grace Christian School Class of 2013. Her hobbies include running, skiing, adventuring with her labradoodle, music, and art. Her favorite Alaskan sceneries are mountains (from both the bottom and top), waterfalls, sunsets, and mudflats. She aspires to write more novels, vanquish armies of snow monsters, and take a few naps in the near future.

Check out these other exciting titles from *Thrive Christian Press*:

Chronicles of the Imagination: Staranana – Enhanced:
ISBN 978-0-9800600-0-3

After enduring centuries under a vicious tyrant, the people of the icy planet Staranana must decide whether to abandon their faith or continue to trust in the promises of God. The results of that decision will spark an adventure beyond the imagination! This enhanced edition includes sneak previews and educational extras great for use in the classroom.

Chronicles of the Imagination: Lizard Face:
ISBN 978-0-9800600-3-4

A time of peace has dawned, but on the eve of the first Christmas on Staranana an ancient enemy returns. Faith, friendship, and family will all be tested, and a single wrong decision could very well spell the doom of Staranana!

Chronicles of the Imagination: Nana-Old Testament
ISBN 978-0-9800600-6-5

The Starananians find themselves stranded in Earth's biblical past, and if they are to find their way home, they'll have to enlist the help of some of the greatest characters from throughout the *Old Testament*.

Chronicles of the Imagination: Nana-New Testament
ISBN 978-0-9800600-7-2

Lost, alone, and homesick, the Starananians continue their journey through the biblical past. They have only one final hope of getting home, and His name is…Jesus Christ.

Find them all today at www.thrivechristianpress.com in both paperback as well as on Amazon Kindle.

www.ingramcontent.com/pod-product-compliance
Lightning Source LLC
Chambersburg PA
CBHW070849120626
46556CB00002B/931